# THE CHRONICLES OF MARITUA

## A NEW ERA

FERRONIC

PenAime
Where AI Meets Stories

The Chronicles of Maritua: A New Era
Published by PenAime Private Ltd
care@penaime.com
www.penaime.com

The characters and events portrayed in this book are fictitious. Any similarity to real persons, living or dead, is coincidental and not intended by the author.

This work was generated with the assistance of Artificial Intelligence (AI) tools including but not limited to Open AI's ChatGPT and Google's Gemini. Copyright protection under applicable laws may apply to the extent that the work contains original human input



ISBN: 978-81-988541-6-2

# A Tribute to Writers: The Architects of Imagination

PenAime does not intend to replace creativity. We respect art and artists. This is only an attempt to support people who require the assistance of AI to bring their ideas to light. We are fully aware that no such technology would have come into existence if not for people who have dedicated their lives to writing and literature.

This is a tribute to every storyteller who has ever dared to put pen to paper, to every voice that has carried meaning across generations. Your words inspire, ignite, and shape the world far beyond any algorithm's reach. And as long as there are minds that weave stories, the written word will remain indomitable—a legacy carried not by machines, but by the souls of those who create.

# PROLOGUE

## A Whisper in the Heart of the Island

Luca Zarek was standing on the long, sparkling bridge to his school when he felt the whole world flinch.

It wasn't a big, rumbling earthquake. It was smaller, quieter, and much weirder. It felt like the entire island of Maritua, which was alive with magic, had just skipped a heartbeat. The feeling zipped up from the bottom of Luca's boots and settled in his tummy like a cold, wiggling worm of worry.

He stopped, and his breath made a little white cloud in the chilly air. Down below, the great River of Magic, which flowed like the island's own blood, seemed to get stuck for a second. The air, which usually crackled with the zizz and pop of spells, went completely silent. And that silence was the scariest part of all.

This was the latest weird thing to happen. For the past few days, spooky stories had been bouncing around the halls of the Grand Academia like magical bouncy balls. The whispers started two days ago. They said that way out in the snowy lands of Frostvale, a royal snow-lynx—a giant, beautiful cat with fur as white as a cloud—had been found frozen.

But it wasn't frozen in ice. It was trapped inside a perfectly clear crystal, caught in the middle of a mighty pounce. Its claws were out, its teeth were bared, and its powerful muscles were ready to spring. The storytellers said there wasn't a single mark on it, not even a paw print in the snow nearby. It was as if the lynx had forgotten how to be alive, and all its life had been instantly swapped for cold, dead crystal. The Queen of Frostvale, Queen Vega, told everyone it was just a strange, natural thing. But the students whispered that the look on her face was not calm; it was terrified.

Then, yesterday, the wrongness came closer. It came right to their school. A first-year student named Elara, a girl with a big, happy laugh who was known for making potions that often exploded with cheerful pink goo, was found lying on the grass in the sky-gardens. The only person who saw what happened was crying and shaking. He said Elara had picked up a creepy piece of black rock, like a sliver of darkest night. He said the rock seemed to pulse with a cold, hungry feeling, as if it wanted to eat the light.

Now, Elara was in a deep, deep sleep in the Tower of Lyra, the best magical hospital in the world. And even the most powerful healers couldn't wake her up. They were baffled. They whispered that her own magic, which used to be warm and green like a summer forest, now felt sick. And they said that if you looked very closely into her unseeing eyes, you could see a faint, strange, purple light flickering inside. A light that felt like it was drinking all the happiness out of the room.

The crystal lynx was a scary story. Elara was a sad one. But this flinch, this skipped heartbeat of the island itself, felt different. It felt like a message.

"Did you feel that?" Luca whispered, but his words were eaten up by the strange quiet. He spun around, hoping to see his friends Iris and Zenith. But the long, sparkling bridge was empty. He was all alone.

The only sound was a low hum, as if the giant island was taking a shaky breath, trying to get its heartbeat right again.

But Luca felt something else, too. He felt a cold, old feeling deep inside him, like a secret waking up after a long, long nap. A feeling of dread that tasted like forgotten things.

And then, from a silent, secret place where the island's heart beat, a voice that wasn't a real voice at all whispered a single word.

It whispered his name.

# Chapter 1: The Whispering Glass and the Forgotten Feather

"A *memory is a tricky thing. It can be a warm blanket or a sharp stone. Sometimes, it's both at once."*

Luca Zarek often sought refuge at the Whispering Glass, a place where the world's noise faded to a murmur. It wasn't the chatter of students or the melodic chime of lecture halls that he fled from, but the relentless clamor inside his own head. It was the persistent, nagging whisper of inadequacy that followed him like a shadow, a voice that told him he was an ordinary boy in a world of wonders, a C-rank talent in a sea of A-rank prodigies. Here, at the edge of the world, he could almost pretend it wasn't true.

The Whispering Glass was a fractured dome of silver-mirrored stone, clinging to a cliffside high above the academy's eastern gardens. Legends claimed it was a fallen star, shattered upon impact, its pieces forever catching the light and reflecting a thousand different versions of the sky. It was a place for secrets and solitude, a place where one could feel small against the vastness of the sea and sky, and find a strange comfort in it.

His fingers, stained with the faint, stubborn blue of practice-glyph ink, absently traced the outline of a strange rune etched deep into the stone beside him. It was shaped like a stylized feather, its delicate barbs intertwined with a complex sigil he'd never seen in any textbook. The carving was ancient, its edges softened by centuries of salt-laced wind, yet something about it felt deeply, personally familiar. A jolt, like the island's earlier flinch, went through him. The unsettling part, the part that made the hairs on his arms stand up, was the handwriting. The elegant, looping flow of the lines looked exactly like his own.

He snatched his hand back as if the stone were hot. He had no memory of ever being here before today, let alone carving a symbol of such impossible design. He tried to rationalize it, to dismiss it as a strange coincidence, a trick of the light on the weathered stone. But the feeling of recognition was a cold, hard knot tightening in his stomach. It felt like remembering a dream he was certain he'd never had.

"Still haunted by the pulse?"

Luca jumped, his heart hammering against his ribs. He turned to see Iris Velden leaning against a crumbling archway, her arms folded across her chest. Her dark braids, intricately woven with threads of shimmering silver, danced in the wind, and her silhouette was a sharp, confident cut against the pale morning light. Her voice was casual, light and teasing, but her eyes—the color of warm amber—were sharp and intelligent. They missed nothing. She had felt the island's tremor, he knew. In her own way, she felt everything.

Luca didn't answer immediately, his gaze drawn back to the impossible rune. "It wasn't just a pulse," he said, his voice barely a whisper. "It was... something else. Like the island flinched away from something." He flexed his fingers. The hand that had traced the rune still tingled with a strange, residual energy.

A second voice, smoother and more self-assured, cut through the quiet. "Come on, you two. Professor Lian won't wait for another 'the-island-has-indigestion' excuse. Some of us actually plan on passing our mid-terms." Zenith Cael descended the worn stone steps with an easy grace, his dark, tailored academy coat flicking around his ankles. His posture was perfect, his expression a carefully constructed mask of effortless control. He was the model student, the prodigy whose magic was as sharp and clear as his ambition. He was their friend, but sometimes he felt like a reminder of everything Luca wasn't.

Iris smirked, playfully nudging Luca with her shoulder and breaking his trance. "Let's go, heartbeat boy."

As they walked the crystalline path that spiraled down toward the heart of the academy, the full, breathtaking majesty of their school revealed itself. The Grand Academia of Nebula was not a building in the traditional sense; it was a living miracle suspended in the sky, a testament to Maritua's unique magic. A central spire of shimmering stone and enchanted alloy stretched into the clouds, so tall it seemed to scratch the belly of the sky. Around this central nexus, twenty-seven smaller towers coiled like metallic vines, connected by shimmering bridges that adapted their shape with every gust of wind.

Floating lecture halls, great spheres of enchanted glass, orbited the main spire like patient moons, their interiors filled with the ghostly glow of projected star-charts and historical timelines. Silent blink-platforms—ribbons of pure, condensed light—glided up and down the spire's spine, ferrying students between the levitating terraces with a soft, melodic hum. Beneath their boots, runes set into the crystalline path flickered to life, syncing with their unique magical auras and guiding them with a gentle, psychic pull. The air itself was a tapestry of smells: the clean, sharp scent of ozone from a nearby elemental lab, the rich aroma of roasting poraleaf from the dining halls, and the ever-present, ink-and-old-parchment smell of a million magical scrolls.

This wasn't just *a* school. It was *the* school. And earning a place here had been the single most terrifying and exhilarating moment of Luca's life.

"Do you remember the day we got in?" Iris asked, her voice softer now, tinged with nostalgia.

Luca managed a faint smile, the memory pushing back his current anxieties. "How could I forget? My hands were shaking so hard I couldn't read the acceptance scroll."

"Pretty sure you cried," Zenith added, the teasing glint back in his eyes.

"I did not," Luca scoffed, though he could feel a betraying warmth creep up his neck.

"You totally did," Iris chuckled, her laughter as bright and clear as a ringing bell. "When they posted the final ranks, you just stood there, staring, looking like you were about to faint. Your parents had come all the way from the tranquil forests of Viridawn, and your mom had to hold you up."

"I was ten," Luca defended himself, unable to suppress a small smile. "And it wasn't just one test. It was an ordeal."

He was right. The Grand Academia didn't select students on magical potential alone. Every child of Maritua, at the age of ten, had to pass the grueling Threefold Trial. First was the Soul Crystal Test, where a child would place their hand on a large, raw ley-crystal. A bright glow meant a strong affinity, while a faint one, like Luca's, suggested a more modest power level. Second was the Intellect Circuit, a labyrinth of mind-bending puzzles and logic traps designed to measure cognition and problem-solving under intense pressure. The final, and many said most important, test was the Temperament Gauge, a deep soul-read performed by a senior instructor that revealed a student's emotional resilience, empathy, and, above all, their capacity for control.

Many children with powerful auras failed, their raw magic deemed too volatile or their tempers too unstable. Others with a weaker spark, like Luca, passed because they showed something the academy valued more: a steady will, a clear mind, and a heart that resonated with the island's gentler frequencies.

"I barely made it through the aptitude rounds," Luca admitted. "I still have nightmares about the pattern glyphs. But you," he said, looking at Iris, "you just charged straight into the puzzle dome like it was a new playground."

"I thought it *was* a playground," she grinned, completely unabashed. "All those lights and moving parts? It was fun! Still passed, didn't I?"

"Of course, you did," Zenith said, though his smile didn't quite reach his eyes. His own acceptance had been a foregone conclusion. The Cael family was old blood in Nebula, with a long line of powerful mages and council members. For him, the Threefold Trial wasn't a challenge; it was a confirmation of his birthright. "Control is everything. Without it, power is just a tantrum."

Their friendly banter was cut short as they arrived at Professor Lian Corvale's lecture hall. The room was already humming with the quiet energy of focused study. At the head of the room, a crystalline board projected a shimmering, three-dimensional map of Maritua's five great realms.

Professor Lian entered in a coat of twilight blue, her movements precise and her gaze missing nothing. She possessed a quiet, unshakable power that commanded more respect than any shouted order. "Up. Grab your satchels," she said, her voice crisp and clear. "We're moving."

Without a word of complaint, the class followed her out of the hall and onto one of the vast outdoor training terraces. It was a wide, circular arena ringed by ancient, weathered sigils, overlooking the shimmering lake far below.

"Magic without meaning is just noise," she stated, her steps silent on the sigil-etched stone as she paced before them. "Power without memory is just dust. This island, Maritua, was not built. It awakened. Its soul breathes in the rock and flows in the water. Every piece of your training is tied to that fundamental truth."

She raised a hand, and a small, glowing crystal, a miniature of the one used in the entrance trials, shimmered above her palm. "You all passed the trials because the Soulstream recognized something in you. You each hold a resonance grade, a measure of your innate connection to the island's magic. Let me remind you what they mean."

Her gaze swept over them, sharp and penetrating, and every student straightened to their full height.

"**E, a Fragile Flame**—unstable, unpredictable, and often dangerous magic. Very rare.

**D, a Flickering Spark**—a faint glow, but no real flare. Requires immense effort to master.

**C, a Kindled Ember**—common, controllable, and dependable. The backbone of our society.

**B, a Flaring Core**—strong, adaptable, and with significant potential for growth.

**A, a Burning Will**—exceptionally powerful and creative. The mark of our great leaders and innovators.

And finally, **S, Soulforged**—a legendary resonance, so rare it is considered myth. Shaped not by power, but by prophecy and destiny itself."

She let the words hang in the air, a tangible weight. "What matters is not where you start—it's how you shape the magic you hold. It is about attunement, a deep connection to the island's pulse. A mage here doesn't just cast a spell; they coax Maritua's energy through their own will. Now... show me."

The field buzzed with nervous energy. "Shape a shield," Professor Lian called out. "Draw from within. Let your aura speak."

Iris stepped into a dueling circle opposite Luca, cracking her knuckles with a grin. "You're up."

Luca took a deep breath, trying to calm the familiar flutter of anxiety in his chest. He focused, picturing the glyphs, pulling on his inner reserves. But the energy wouldn't mold. It spiked, sharp and sudden, and his control shattered like glass. Theshield he'd envisioned collapsed into a pathetic puff of blue smoke, and the defensive rune beneath his feet cracked with a disheartening fizzle. A few students nearby snickered.

"Still cute," Iris teased gently, her own shimmering, crescent-shaped shield holding steady and effortless, a perfect construct of golden light. "Even when you're failing spectacularly."

Luca groaned, running a hand through his messy hair. "I'm going to turn your spellbooks into slugs."

Nearby, Zenith's shield was flawless, a perfect dome of white light that pulsed with unwavering, disciplined strength. He made it look as easy as breathing. As Luca watched, a familiar wave of frustration washed over him. Why was it so hard for him, and so simple for them?

Later, as they sat on the cool grass, catching their breath, Professor Lian stopped beside Luca. He tensed, expecting a lecture on his lack of control.

"Your magic doesn't fail, Mr. Zarek," she said quietly, her sharp eyes seeming to look right through him into something deeper. "It's just not ready to be caged. You try to force it into a shape it does not know. Try listening to it instead."

Before Luca could begin to puzzle out her cryptic words, a sudden hush fell over the training ground. Every eye, every face, turned to the sky.

From high in the clouds, a single, jet-black feather drifted down. It wasn't falling so much as descending, spiraling slowly as if suspended on an invisible thread. It trailed faint, ethereal violet sparks, like lazy, sleeping fireflies. It felt ancient, out of place, a piece of a story no one remembered reading.

Instinctively, without thought or reason, Luca reached out his hand. The feather, guided by some unseen current, landed gently in the center of his palm. It was strangely warm to the touch and seemed to hum with a faint, inner energy—the echo of a forgotten flight. He looked at Iris, then at Zenith. Their teasing expressions were gone, replaced by a shared look of awe and profound unease.

"Did you feel that?" Luca whispered, the words echoing his earlier question on the bridge, but this time, he knew they had.

Zenith didn't answer. He was staring at the horizon, his jaw tight, his expression unreadable.

Then, the world shifted. It was a sensation that rippled through everyone on the terrace, a collective gasp of disbelief. The sun didn't flicker. The sky didn't tremble.

*It blinked.*

For one, silent, soul-stopping heartbeat, the light of the world went out and came back on, as if a giant eye had closed and opened again. And in that moment of absolute stillness, everyone knew, with a certainty that was colder than any winter wind, that something was about to break.

# Chapter 2: The Grand Archive and the Last Ash

"A *secret is a weight. The longer you carry it, the more it changes your shape."*

The black feather in Luca's palm pulsed with a silent, secret rhythm, a beat that seemed to echo the flinch he'd felt in the island's core. The violet sparks clinging to its edge were not a magic he recognized from any class; they were more like memories dressed as light, tiny embers of a forgotten fire that curled upwards before winking out of existence.

"No bird on this island glows like that," Iris said, her voice a low murmur. She crouched beside him, her usual boundless confidence replaced by a focused, analytical curiosity. Her eyes, sharp and perceptive, traced the feather's impossible design. "Unless it's cursed... or something much, much older."

"History is filled with things we've chosen to forget," Zenith added, his tone unusually thoughtful. He wasn't looking at the feather as a simple curiosity, but as a problem, a puzzle to be dissected and solved. "Sometimes, they find a way to remind us."

The bell chimed, signaling the end of the training session, but no one moved. The image of the sky blinking was burned into their minds. Professor Lian dismissed the class with a curt, worried nod, her own composure visibly shaken. The mystery of the feather was too pressing to ignore. By silent, mutual agreement, the trio made their way not to the dining hall, but to the Grand Archive.

The Archive was a spiraling marvel of enchanted glass and silver-veined stone, a place that felt as ancient as Maritua itself. Six massive, flawless ley-crystals floated in a slow, majestic orbit above its highest peak, humming with the untapped knowledge of generations. Inside, the air was cool and still, filled with the comforting scent of old parchment, leather bindings, and the faint, clean crackle of preservation spells. Spiral walkways, enchanted to move with a slow, hypnotic grace, spun around a glowing central pillar—the Archive's ley-heart, a colossal crystal that pulsed with the collected memories and knowledge of Maritua. It was said that if you pressed your ear to the crystal, you could hear the whispers of every story ever told on the island.

As they stepped inside, a subtle pressure settled on their shoulders, the distinct feeling of being observed, of the very walls learning their names and weighing their intentions. It was a place of immense power, and it demanded respect.

Near a half-lit balcony overlooking the lower tiers, a boy sat alone in a high-backed velvet chair. He was engrossed in a thick, leather-bound tome that rested in his lap, his fingers tracing the gilded letters on its spine. He wore the standard academy uniform, but his was tailored from a finer, jet-black cloth, with silver-lined cuffs that seemed to absorb the light. On his shoulder shimmered a circular silver insignia, intricately threaded with a single, brilliant blue flame. It wasn't a house crest or a class rank. It was something else entirely, something that spoke of a hidden order or a profound achievement.

"That symbol," Luca whispered, nodding discreetly in the boy's direction. "Have you seen it before?"

Iris narrowed her eyes, her gaze sharp. "No. But the embroidery is hand-stitched with silver ley-thread. That's custom work, and expensive. That's no regular academy badge."

Zenith stared a moment longer, his analytical gaze taking in every detail of the boy's posture and the quiet confidence he radiated. "He's not just an upperclassman," Zenith concluded, his voice low. "That's someone under watch. Or someone doing the watching."

The boy didn't look up, didn't even seem to notice their presence. But the slow, deliberate way he turned a page, without making a single sound, made the vast space around him feel smaller, calmer, and far more dangerous.

Pushing the encounter from their minds, the trio began their search. Luca, ever the diligent student, pulled a heavy, dust-covered book from a high shelf: *Magical Avians of Maritua, Sixth Edition*. He carried it to a reading table, the enchanted pages glowing faintly as he opened it. He flipped through the detailed illustrations. "Skywhales... Emberdrakes... Whispergulls... Crystal-crested Moas... nothing here mentions solid black feathers with violet, memory-like trails."

Iris, meanwhile, was cross-referencing books on magical artifacts and curses. "There are mentions of 'shadow-feathers' in some older texts, but they're described as cold, draining life force. This," she said, looking at the feather, which Luca had placed on the table, "feels warm. Alive."

"Maybe it's not from a creature at all," Zenith suggested, leaning against a bookshelf, his arms folded. "Maybe it's older than that. A remnant. An echo of something that no longer exists."

Luca sighed in frustration and closed the heavy book, sending a puff of enchanted dust motes dancing into a sunbeam. "Whatever it is, I don't think we'll find it in a book." He carefully wrapped the feather in a clean piece of parchment from his satchel and tucked it away, placing it next to the small, personal ley-crystal he used for focusing his magic during practice.

As he did, a faint, almost invisible wisp of violet light slipped from the feather and was absorbed into the crystal. It was as quiet and subtle as a secret finding a new home, a seed of shadow planted in a stone of light. None of them noticed it.

Later that day, in the massive Training Dome, a new professor stood at the center of the arena. He was a tall, imposing man in midnight-blue robes, etched with the faded sigils of old combat spells that traced his sleeves like well-worn scars.

"I am Professor Ilaren," he said, his voice calm but carrying an undeniable weight that silenced the murmuring students. "I teach Combat Strategy and Elemental Precision. As you may have heard, there is a Trial of Ascent approaching—an interschool match. For the first time in the history of this academy, first-year initiates will be permitted to compete."

A wave of shocked whispers broke the stillness, rippling through the assembled students.

"You will be matched against the chosen champions from Frostvale, Lunareth, Dravemire, and Viridawn," Ilaren continued, his gaze sweeping over them. "This is not about earning medals or house points. The Council is concerned about the growing instability of the island. This trial is a test of raw skill, of resilience, of spirit. They are looking for answers, and they believe they might find them in the untapped potential of Maritua's youngest and brightest."

Luca's eyes widened. This was unprecedented. The tremors, the crystalized lynx, Elara, the blinking sky... it was all connected. The island's leaders were scared. Zenith's gaze flicked to Iris, who, after a moment of stunned silence, broke into a wide, fierce, and slightly terrifying grin.

"Well," she said, cracking her knuckles with an audible pop. "Let's go ruin someone's week."

As evening fell and the sky turned a deep shade of bruised purple, Luca returned to his dorm room alone. He opened his locker to put away his books and froze, his blood running cold.

The parchment he had so carefully wrapped the feather in was gone.

In its place, his personal ley-crystal, usually a calm and steady blue, was glowing with a sickly, vibrant violet. A web of thin, hairline cracks spiderwebbed across its surface, pulsing with a light that was not his own. It felt alive. It felt *hungry*.

He reached for it, his rational mind screaming at him not to, but an irresistible pull drew his fingers forward. The moment his skin touched the corrupted crystal, his world shattered into a million pieces.

*Pulse.*

His body remained standing by the open locker, but his mind plummeted into a vision—vast, silent, and screaming with unspoken horror. He stood on scorched earth under a sky choked with red ash. The land itself wept, bleeding a dark, corrupted energy from gaping wounds. And in the center of the devastation stood five figures, silhouetted by flame and fury. Four of them he recognized instantly from the grand statues in Nebula's Central Plaza—the founding heroes of Maritua, their forms twisted into nightmarish parodies.

But the fifth... the fifth was new. It was cloaked in shifting shadows, its face a featureless void. And emblazoned across its back, burning with a cold, violet fire that matched the light in his crystal, was a sigil.

The sigil of a stylized feather. The exact same symbol carved into the stone at the Whispering Glass.

Then the vision was gone.

Luca blinked, finding himself sprawled on the floor of his room, his heart hammering as if it wanted to escape his chest. His locker stood open. The ley-crystal sat on the shelf, back to its normal, calm blue, the cracks vanished as if they had never existed. The feather was gone. But something remained. An echo. A strange, tingling warmth in his right palm, where the real feather had rested.

Something ancient. Something that was now a part of him.

Across the campus, in the dueling dome, a roar of applause erupted. Dozens of students leaned over the railings, their faces a mixture of shock and admiration. In the center of the arena stood the boy from the archive, Riven Solis. His black coat billowed slightly in the aftermath of a powerful spell. On his shoulder, the silver crest with the blue flame seemed to pulse with its own inner light. He had just moved like lightning wrapped in silk, disarming a highly-ranked third-year student with insulting, almost casual, ease.

Up in the stands, Luca, who had rushed out of his room seeking the comforting noise of others, leaned forward. "It's *him*," he whispered to Iris and Zenith, who had joined him.

Riven glanced up, his gaze sweeping across the crowd. For a single, charged moment, his eyes—sharp, knowing, and impossibly old—met Luca's. He gave a faint, almost imperceptible nod, an acknowledgment that passed between them like a secret. Then he turned and walked away, melting back into the shadows of the academy as if he were one of them.

Later that night, long after the moon had risen, Riven knelt in an abandoned, overgrown wing of the academy shrine. He knelt before a small, hidden alcove, nearly consumed by moss and time. A single name was carved there, the letters worn and faded: *Lyra*. It was not the name of the great Healer of Lunareth, but another. He gently placed a folded piece of paper on the cold stone—a crude child's drawing of two stick figures holding hands under a lopsided sun.

"I'm sorry," he whispered to the sleeping stones, his voice cracking on the single, broken word. A faint, blue-white magic, the same color as the flame on his crest, shimmered on his hands before curling back into his skin, a grief too powerful to be released. He stood, his eyes sharp and hollow. Not empty. Just... waiting.

And in his own room, Luca sat on the edge of his bed, staring at his empty right palm. The feather was gone, but the warmth remained. It wasn't a memory of its touch. Thewarmth was coming from *him*.

He didn't know what it meant. But he knew, with a certainty that chilled him to the bone, that for the first time in his life, when he looked into the darkness, something ancient was looking back. And it had just called him by name.

# Chapter 3: The Silence in Her Wake

*"The heaviest silences are not empty. They are full of the words we can no longer say."*

In Maritua, mornings always pretended that nothing had ever been broken. Sunlight spilled across the academy grounds like a silent, golden forgiveness, and the ancient sigils set in the cobblestone paths hummed their soft, peaceful tune. But for Iris Velden, the peace was a thin veneer over a terrifying quiet. It was the quiet that now lived in the space beside her, the quiet that had once been filled with the chaotic, brilliant, and fiercely loyal presence of Kaelin.

The change had been gradual at first, a slow dimming of Kaelin's inner light. It had started the day her childhood friend, Elara, had touched the Hollow Shard. Iris had gone with Kaelin to the Tower of Lyra, the island's main healing sanctum, a place that was usually a beacon of hope and warmth. But the room where Elara lay was cold. A strange, faint violet light flickered deep within the comatose girl's eyes, and the air around her felt thin and hungry, as if it were drinking the life from the very stones. The Healers, their faces grim, spoke in hushed tones of a "soul-corruption" they had no remedy for.

Kaelin had stood by Elara's bedside, holding her friend's limp hand, her face a mask of pale determination. From that day on, she was a different person. Her usual vibrant energy was replaced by a frantic, nervous buzz. She spent every spare moment in the Grand Archive, not in the bright, open sections with the other students, but in the dusty, forgotten lower levels where the forbidden texts were kept under lock and key.

A few days ago, Iris had found her there, tucked away in a shadowy alcove, surrounded by stacks of books with titles like *Anomalous Ley-Resonances* and *The Veil of Echoes*. Kaelin had looked up, startled, her eyes wide and haunted. A half-dozen scrolls were spread before her, covered in frantic, overlapping notes about "Hollow Shards" and "memory echoes." On one, she had sketched a crude but familiar drawing—a stylized feather, identical to the one that had fallen from the sky.

"Kaelin, what is all this?" Iris had asked, her voice soft with concern. "You look like you haven't slept in days."

Kaelin had quickly rolled up the scrolls, forcing a laugh that sounded brittle and hollow. "Oh, you know. Just some extra credit for Professor Ilaren. He's obsessed with ancient curses. Super boring stuff." She had grabbed Iris's arm, pulling her away from the shadowy alcove. "Come on, let's go get some glimmerfruit toast. My brain is turning to dust."

But Iris had seen the truth in her friend's eyes. It wasn't the thrill of research that lit them up; it was pure, undiluted fear.

That fear had been present yesterday morning, in their last conversation. Kaelin had stood by the window, staring out at the distant, shimmering capital of Nebula, her usual cheerful chatter conspicuously absent. Then, she had turned, her expression uncharacteristically serious, and pressed the silver pendant into Iris's hand. It was a memory-locket, a simple but powerful charm that held a psychic echo of a shared moment. Iris could feel the memory contained within: the two of them as first-years, hiding in a closet after accidentally turning a professor's robes into a flock of angry geese, their shoulders shaking with suppressed laughter.

"Figured you deserved something real," Kaelin had said, her voice strangely soft. "Since you keep saving the parts of me that always try to drift off." She had attempted a grin, but it was a sad, fragile thing. "Besides," she'd added, her joking mask slipping back on, "it doesn't explode, so it's already an improvement on that fireproof quill case from first year."

Iris had smiled, a real, warm smile, and fastened the pendant around her neck, the familiar warmth of the memory a comfort against her skin. But looking back, she saw the scene for what it was. It wasn't a gift. It was a goodbye.

Now, standing in the middle of their dorm room, the silence was a physical weight. Iris had returned from her classes to find the room too quiet, too still. Kaelin's bed, usually a chaotic nest of blankets, books, and half-finished projects, was neatly made. That alone was a blaring alarm bell. Her favorite scarf, a colorful monstrosity she'd knitted herself, still hung from the bedpost, fluttering gently in the breeze from the open window. A half-full glass of water sat on her nightstand, condensation beading on its side.

And next to it was an open glyphbook. Its pages were filled with Kaelin's frantic, looping script, detailing everything she had found. There were notes about the Hollow Shards being fragments of a place called "the Fold," a dimension of memory. There were terrifying passages about echoes that could "wear" the faces of the lost. And there were dozens of sketches of the feather sigil, circled again and again.

Resting on the pillow, catching a single, lonely ray of moonlight, was the other pendant. Kaelin's.

Iris's breath caught in her throat. She approached the bed slowly, as if it were a wild animal that might bolt. Her fingers hovered over the cool metal, a cold dread creeping into her heart. It felt too final, a period at the end of a sentence she wasn't ready to finish reading. She picked it up. Beneath it lay a note, folded once. Perfectly.

Kaelin never folded anything perfectly.

That's how Iris knew it was real. Her hands trembling so badly she could barely hold the paper, she unfolded it.

*Iris,*

*There are some pages that shouldn't be read. I turned one too many. The whispers they heard from Elara weren't just dreams. They're echoes from a place called the Fold. And they're hungry.*

*The feather is a key. The violet light is a door. I think I know how to close it, but I have to do it from the other side. Don't let them follow me. Don't look for me. I need to be the last one through.*

*Don't forget me.*

*K.*

The note slipped from her fingers, fluttering to the floor like a dead leaf. *What did you do?* Iris whispered to the empty room, her voice breaking. *You idiot. You brave, stupid idiot.*

Thunder cracked, but only in her memory. A few nights ago, during a raging thunderstorm, Kaelin had dragged her out to the training yards. She had danced in the rain, her arms wide, her face turned to the sky, daring the lightning to strike her.

"If I vanish," she'd laughed, her voice bright and wild, her clothes soaked and shining, "at least let it be dramatic! Promise you'll tell everyone I was taken by a dragon!"

Iris had rolled her eyes, hiding her own smile. "You'd probably leave a pun in your ashes."

Now, the silence in the room thundered louder than any storm. It was a silence filled with the shape of her best friend, with the ghost of her laughter and the weight of her sacrifice.

The next day, Iris moved through the academy like a phantom, the world muted and gray. The sound of laughter in the Great Hall felt like a personal insult, a jarring note in the funereal symphony of her grief. She sat with Luca and Zenith, but their worried words were a distant, meaningless buzz. She saw that Luca looked haunted, too, his eyes shadowed with secrets he wasn't sharing. She saw Zenith's coiled frustration, his ambition a shield against a world that was suddenly, frighteningly, not going according to his plan. But their problems felt small, insignificant next to the gaping hole that had been torn in her own world.

That night, back in the crushing silence of her room, Iris sat at her desk, holding both silver pendants in her palm. They were still warm, not like metal, but like a held hand, a memory refusing to let go. Kaelin's laugh echoed in her mind, not with joy, but like the crackle of distant lightning, a warning of the storm that had already arrived and stolen everything.

In that moment, staring at the empty bed across the room, its perfect neatness a constant, screaming accusation, Iris made a promise to the silence. Her grief was a cold, hard stone in her chest, but beneath it, something new was kindling. It was hot and sharp and bright. It was rage.

This wasn't over. Not until the whispers that had taken her friend became screams.

And Iris Velden was ready to scream back.

# Chapter 4: Ash in the Mirror

"T*he greatest weakness is not the fear of falling, but the belief that you are not strong enough to rise."*

That night, Luca's dreams weren't dreams at all. They were a trial. He didn't drift into sleep; he plunged into a cold, black silence, landing with a jarring thud on a floor of polished, obsidian-like stone. He was in a vast, vaulted chamber with no windows and no doors, the air thick with the scent of ozone and regret. And he was not alone.

He was facing himself.

Or rather, something that wore his shape. This other Luca was older, not in years, but in weariness. His shoulders were slumped in defeat, his eyes were hollow, empty voids that held no light, and his hands dripped with a glistening, dark red liquid that wasn't blood. It was shame.

The mirror version of him smiled, a cruel, twisted thing that held no warmth. *"You disappoint even yourself,"* it whispered, its voice a venomous echo of Luca's own deepest insecurities.

Then, it lunged.

Luca raised his hand to cast a defensive glyph, the motions second nature from a thousand failed attempts in the training yard. But the magic sputtered and died before it could form. The air refused to listen to him. His mouth opened to speak an incantation, but the words caught in his throat, turning to ash on his tongue. His body, his magic, his very will had abandoned him.

The mirror-Luca didn't hesitate. Its punch was not a physical blow, but a strike of pure, concentrated failure that sent him crashing to the stone floor. The impact drove the air from his lungs and filled his mind with a cacophony of his worst memories: the snickering of his classmates, the disappointed sigh of a professor, the worried look in his parents' eyes.

He looked up, gasping for breath, and the chamber around him shifted. Across the vault, he saw Kaelin. She was alive, whole, and smiling her bright, crooked smile. She looked at him, and her smile faded, replaced by a look of profound pity. Then, she turned and walked away, each footstep leaving a soft, soundless pile of gray ash behind, like snow burning in reverse.

Zenith was there, too. He stood silently, his perfect posture radiating disapproval. He met Luca's desperate gaze, then simply vanished, not even bothering with a farewell.

The mirror behind them fractured, and voices spilled through the cracks—Kaelin's laughter, Iris's teasing, Zenith's cool confidence. But the voices were distorted, layered with a mocking cruelty. *"Heartbeat boy." "Still can't cast?" "Useless." "Weak."*

One voice rose louder than the rest, his own voice, filled with a despair that was as deep as the sea. *"You were never ready to stand. You only ever watch as others fall."*

Thevault floor began to ripple like liquid glass, shimmering with broken glyphs and the impossible, violet-tinged sigil of the feather. Iris's new pendant, the one Kaelin had made for her, floated there for a single, heartbreaking breath. Then it sank into the shimmering red floor with a sound like a choking gasp.

Luca reached for it, a desperate cry finally tearing from his throat.

And woke up.

He didn't scream. He didn't cry. He just lay in his bed, tangled in his sweat-soaked sheets, staring at his own hands as if they belonged to a stranger. The dream-blood had vanished, but the shame hadn't. It was a cold, heavy cloak he couldn't shrug off. The world outside his window was a wall of gray, oppressive clouds, the kind that promised a storm that would never break.

The Hall of Sigils was colder than usual that morning, or maybe the chill was just inside him. Luca sat hunched at his desk, staring at a blank piece of parchment. He had tried—again—to practice a simple warming glyph, and had failed—again. The ink had dried on the edge of his hand where his quill had slipped, a testament to his trembling inability. The dream clung to him like frost, the whispers of his mirror-self echoing in his ears.

He saw Iris across the room. Her eyes were red-rimmed and hollow, but she held her head high, a silent, defiant fortress of grief. He saw Zenith, practicing complex spell-chains with a fierce, almost violent, precision, his frustration a palpable aura around him. They were hurting, too. And in that moment, the silence between them felt heavier than his fear.

He walked over to their table and sat down, his movements stiff. His fingers twitched. His lips parted. He was going to say nothing, as usual. He was going to swallow his fear and pretend he was fine, just as he always did.

But this time, he couldn't.

"I had a dream last night," Luca said suddenly, his voice quiet but clear in the relative hush of the hall. "I fought myself. And I lost."

Zenith blinked, lowering the glowing glyph he was weaving in the air. Iris looked up slowly, her hollow-eyed gaze focusing on him for the first time all morning.

Luca took a shaky breath, the confession tumbling out of him now that it had started. "I just... I realized I'm weak. Not just my magic. Me. And I don't want to be. Not anymore." He looked at them, his friends, his expression a raw plea. "I want to train. I want to get stronger. I mean, if you'll help me," he added, his voice cracking slightly. "I know I'm not... like you two. But I have to try."

Zenith stared at him, a flicker of something unreadable in his eyes. But Iris, her expression softening with a flicker of empathy, gave a slow, deliberate nod. "Okay, Luca," she said, her voice rough with unshed tears. "Okay. We'll train."

They went to the training yard, the same one where the black feather had fallen. The old trees surrounding the cracked stone path seemed to watch them with a solemn quiet. Luca stood in the center of a dueling circle, trembling but trying not to show it. He took a deep breath, raised his hands, and channeled. He felt the glyph begin to form, a flicker of hope igniting in his chest...

And then—nothing. The magic dissolved into a pathetic wisp of smoke.

The silence that followed was harder to bear than any laughter. He swallowed the hot, burning shame in his throat. *Not again. Please, not again.*

A few upper-year students walked past, their voices carrying on the wind.

"Is that Zarek? Still can't cast a simple barrier charm?" "Someone get him a practice wand. Or a pillow to cry into."

Luca flinched as if struck. He clenched his fists, his knuckles white, and said nothing.

But Iris did.

"You think this is funny?" Her voice was not loud, but it cut across the yard like a shard of ice. The students turned, one of them smirking. "You think any of this is a joke to you?"

She was already moving. She stepped forward, her fists clenched, not to attack, but to *shield* him. Her grief for Kaelin, her worry for the island, her sudden, fierce protectiveness of the vulnerable boy in front of her—it all coalesced into a single, explosive point.

A sharp *crack* split the air. It wasn't the sound of a spell. It was the sound of something breaking inside Iris.

The ground beneath her feet shook. A sudden, visible wave of raw, untamed pressure burst from her, a pure, unfiltered expression of her pain and rage. It wasn't elegant or controlled. It was a psychic scream given form. The students who had been laughing stumbled back, their faces paling in shock. One of them was thrown against a stone wall with a heavy grunt.

Iris stood frozen in the center of the shockwave she had created, her eyes wide with horror. She hadn't meant to do that. She looked down at her scraped hand, where blood was tracing a thin, red line across her knuckles.

"Get back," Zenith said quickly, stepping in—not aggressive, but calm, steadying. He reached her first, his movements fluid with instinct. "Iris," he said softly, his voice losing its usual arrogant edge. "You're alright. Breathe."

"I didn't mean to," she muttered, her voice cracking. "I just... they don't know. They don't know what it's like to... to lose..." She stopped, unable to say the name. But the pain wasn't just about Luca anymore. It was about Kaelin.

Zenith knelt beside her, his hand hovering over her wrist, his body shielding her from the curious, fearful gazes of the other students. "I know," he said again, his voice gentle. "You've been holding it in for too long."

She shivered, a single tear finally escaping and tracing a path through the grime on her cheek. "I couldn't protect her, Zenith."

He didn't ask who. He didn't need to. He just nodded, as if he understood everything.

Then Luca joined them. He moved slowly, quietly, and sat down in the grass on her other side. He didn't try to say anything comforting. He didn't try to fix it. He just sat with her, a silent, steady presence in the chaos she had barely contained. And she let them, these two boys, her friends, sit on either side of her, their shoulders almost touching hers, grounding her in the storm of her own grief.

For the first time in days, the silence didn't hurt. It was shared.

Later, after the others had left, Zenith remained behind. The cracked earth where Iris had stood still pulsed with a faint, residual energy. He knelt slowly, brushing his hand across the fracture in the stone. In the center of the break, he saw it. The stone hadn't just split. It had been *etched* by the sheer force of her emotion.

Glimmering faintly in the ruined floor were shapes. A crescent moon. A twisted, laughing tree. And two figures beneath it—one holding something small.

Zenith's breath caught. It was the image from Kaelin's pendant.

The crack hadn't just revealed damage. It had revealed a memory. It had revealed her grief.

"This wasn't a spell," he whispered to the empty yard. "She remembered too hard." He stood, a new, unsettling understanding dawning in his eyes. Power wasn't just about control. It was about heart. And he had no idea what to do with that knowledge.

Far beyond the training yards, hidden between light and distance, something watched. Riven Solis. He stood perfectly still, the wind seeming to bend around him. His eyes, which didn't reflect the light but seemed to swallow it, were fixed on the three friends. Then, he didn't vanish. The world simply blinked. And forgot he had ever been there.

# Chapter 5: The Hollowmark and the Keeper

"*Do not fear the darkness in your heart. It is the only part of you that does not lie about the light.*"

That night, Luca didn't fall into a nightmare. He was summoned.

He had been sitting on the edge of his bed, trying to meditate as Professor Lian had suggested, attempting to "listen" to his magic instead of forcing it. He focused on the quiet rhythm of his own breathing, on the distant, steady hum of the Soulstream. And then, another rhythm began to beat alongside it—a deep, violet-red pulse that emanated from his right palm.

The faint, tingling warmth he'd felt since the feather disappeared ignited into a searing heat. He gasped, his eyes flying open. The Hollowmark, the sigil of the feather, was blazing on his skin, not a memory, but a burning, tangible reality. It was a key turning in a lock he hadn't known existed. The world dissolved.

He did not fall. He was *pulled.*

He awoke barefoot on a floor of polished marble, veined with hairline fractures that shimmered like distant, dying galaxies. Embedded in the floor, as far as the eye could see, were feathers—thousands upon thousands of them. But they were not the soft, black feather he had held. Thesewere jagged, obsidian things, streaked with a static, violet energy, each one pulsing with the faint, sorrowful heartbeat of a forgotten memory. The air here was thin and cold, tasting of ozone and borrowed breath. This was the Aetherfold, the place between truth and fear.

A single feather, unlike the others, floated freely in the space before him. In the waking world, the feather he'd touched had been black. Here, its duplicate was a brilliant, ghostly white, its quill glowing from within like a star trapped in glass.

"You have stepped where silence remembers."

The voice was a low, resonant rumble, like distant thunder gathering deep within the earth. It came from everywhere and nowhere at once. A figure emerged from the hazy, violet-tinged air, coalescing as if from thought itself. He was tall and ageless, clad in layered robes of ink and dusk, and silver light threaded through his sleeves in symbols that seemed to twist and writhe, refusing to be deciphered. The man's face was carved in a profound stillness, the face of a being sculpted to witness endings. His eyes were the color of a pale, ancient sky.

"Who... are you?" Luca stammered, taking an involuntary step back.

"I am a keeper," the man said simply. His voice was not unkind, but it held the weight of millennia. "Of echoes. Of truths too tired to speak for themselves. You may call me Elarion."

The white feather drifted upward, and Elarion caught it effortlessly between two long fingers. "This brought you here. A Hollowmark. A key to a door that should have remained locked."

"The feather... in the training yard..." Luca's breath caught.

"Yes," Elarion said, his pale eyes fixed on Luca. "Black in your world. White in this one. That is how the Veil between realms shows its cracks. It inverts what it touches." The Hollowmark shimmered in Elarion's hand, flickering with a breathless, ancient memory.

"Why me?" Luca asked, the question a raw whisper.

Elarion's head tilted slightly. "Because the Aetherfold listens to those who are closest to breaking. It is drawn to doubt. To fear. To the cracks in a soul. And you, Luca Zarek... you echo with them."

Thewords clung to Luca like a cold fog. He shook his head. "I—I didn't mean to come here."

"No one ever does," Elarion replied, his voice resonating with a sad finality. "But the Fold does not ask. It calls. And it demands a toll." The space around them began to twist. The obsidian feathers embedded in the floor rose slowly, forming a great, silent vortex above them. The light dimmed, and the white Hollowmark floated from Elarion's hand, suspended in the air between them.

"What is this place?" Luca whispered, his heart hammering.

"Theplace between what is real and what you fear," Elarion said. "To leave, you must give the Fold something of yourself. Your fear must be given a name. It must have shape."

"You want me to tell you what I'm afraid of?" Luca asked, incredulous.

Elarion said nothing. He only gestured to the floating feather.

The vortex of feathers above them spun faster, a silent, roaring cyclone of forgotten sorrows. One burst into violet flame, and Luca was plunged into a vision.

He saw his mother's hands, her face etched with worry, as she tried to shield him from a wild surge of his own accidental magic when he was a small child. He saw the disappointment in his father's eyes the day he received his C-rank resonance. He saw Iris turning away from him, her face contorted in accusation, her voice whispering, *"You were too slow. You're always too slow."* He saw Zenith shattering a training dummy with a single, perfect blast of energy, then looking at Luca with cold, dismissive pity.

He gasped, the images shattering like glass. A scream clawed its way up his throat—but it wasn't his own. It echoed as if it came from inside the feathers themselves, a chorus of a thousand forgotten failures. And yet, it screamed his name.

Luca fell to his knees, clutching his head. "I don't know what I'm supposed to be," he choked out, the confession tearing from him, raw and honest. "They believe in me—Iris, my parents—but they shouldn't. They see something that isn't there."

The white Hollowmark floated down, hovering just before his face, waiting.

His chest felt as if it were caving in. He clenched his fists, the dream-shame from his nightmare washing over him again.

"I'm afraid I'll always be the one who watches," he said, his voice cracking. "The one who stands by while the people I care about get hurt." He shook his head fiercely. "No... that's not it. That's not the real truth." He looked up, his eyes meeting the empty space where Elarion's should be. "I'm afraid I'll never be fast enough. That I'll only ever survive, never save. I'm afraid that one day, the world will ask me to be a hero, and all I'll be is a witness to the tragedy."

He finally gave the fear its true name. "I'm afraid I'll prove them all right about me."

And then—stillness.

The vortex of feathers slowed, settling back into the marble floor. The oppressive weight in the air lifted. The Hollowmark floated down and gently touched Luca's open palm. He braced himself for a burn, for a searing pain.

But there was none. Instead, a network of faint, violet lines curled across his skin, not a brand of pain, but a map, like roots seeking something hidden deep within him. They were quiet, patient, and permanent. They sank into him, and he knew, with absolute certainty, that they were now part of his soul.

Elarion nodded, a flicker of something like approval in his ancient eyes. "You have named your fear. You have given it its shape. That is enough. For now." He paused, his form beginning to grow translucent. "You think fear is your weakness, Luca Zarek. But it is the only part of you that does not lie. Learn to listen to it."

His voice began to echo, fading as the Aetherfold dissolved around Luca. "Keep this a secret. Speak of the Fold, and it may listen again. Secrets keep their shape. Words give them hunger. And its hunger... is for what you conceal."

Elarion's final words were a mantra etched into the returning silence of Luca's room. *"Truth survives longer than power. It always does."*

And the world went dark.

Luca awoke with a jolt, sitting bolt upright in his bed. The stone walls of his room were cold and solid. Faint morning light filtered through the shutters in hazy stripes. He looked down at his right hand.

It was unmarked.

But he could feel it, just beneath the skin. A door, barely ajar. He stood and walked to the small mirror above his desk. His reflection was pale and shaken, but it was his own. He turned his hand over, and for just a fraction of a second, he saw it—at the edge of his palm, a faint shimmer of violet curled in the shape of a feather before vanishing.

He knew it hadn't left. It had *entered*. And he, and his magic, would never be the same.

# Chapter 6: The Echo of Selection

"D*estiny does not care if you are ready. It simply arrives."*

A palpable tension had settled over the Grand Academia, a chill that had nothing to do with the autumn air sweeping down from the high peaks. The upcoming Trial of Ascent was no longer a subject of excited gossip and friendly wagers. It had become a source of profound anxiety, a great, unknown weight pressing down on the student body. Thenews that first-years were being included for the first time in history had snuffed out the festive atmosphere, replacing it with grim speculation. Everyone knew what it meant: the adults were scared. And when the unshakable leaders of Maritua were scared, it was time for everyone else to be terrified.

Luca felt the knot in his stomach tighten with every passing hour. He had told Iris and Zenith about his vision in the Aetherfold, about Elarion and the warning of the Fold's hunger. Iris, her grief for Kaelin a constant, simmering fire in her eyes, had accepted it without question. She had seen the impossible herself and now believed the world was far darker and more fragile than she had ever imagined. Zenith, however, had been dismissive. He'd listened with a cool, skeptical detachment, attributing Luca's experience to stress or a latent magical surge. "Visions are for prophets and the unstable," he'd said, his words a clean, sharp cut. "We should be focusing on what's real: training, strategy, and strength." The rift between them had become a quiet, aching chasm.

Suddenly, a chime echoed throughout the academy. It was not the gentle, melodic tone of class changes, but a clear, resonant peal that cut through every sound and silenced every conversation. It was a summons. A grand, authoritative voice, laced with magic and broadcast through every spell-stone on campus, boomed across the sky.

"Attention, all students of Nebula Academia! Report immediately to the Resonance Hall. The Selection for the Trial of Ascent will now commence. All years are required to attend. First-year initiates, prepare to be assessed. Only those whose names are called will step forward."

The formality of the announcement was ominous. A sense of dread, cold and heavy, settled over Luca. This was it.

The Resonance Hall was the oldest and most sacred chamber in the Grand Academia, a place reserved for only the most momentous occasions. It was a vast, circular space carved into the central spire, its ceiling so high it seemed to hold its own private sky. Sunlight, filtered through enormous stained-glass windows, painted the floor in vibrant, shifting colors. The windows didn't depict abstract patterns, but the heroic figures of Maritua's past—legendary mages and warriors whose names were whispered with a reverence usually reserved for gods.

The hall was already filled with students from every year, the air thick with the scent of ozone and nervous anticipation. The senior students occupied the higher, tiered balconies, their expressions ranging from detached curiosity to intense scrutiny. They would be witnesses, but their part in this was over. In the center of the hall, on a raised dais of black, unadorned stone, was not an obelisk or a crystal, but a swirling, shimmering pool of pure, liquid light. It was the Resonance Pool, a direct conduit to the Soulstream, and its power made the hairs on Luca's arms stand on end.

At the heart of the Hall stood Chancellor Caelen, a tall, statuesque woman whose presence was a quiet but absolute force. Her silver hair was bound with threads of obsidian glyph-ribbon, and her indigo robes were stitched with constellations that shimmered subtly as she moved. Her eyes, the color of polished moonstone, swept across the assembled students—not observing, but weighing. She was not merely the academy's highest authority; she was the living embodiment of its ancient laws.

And she was not alone. On a high gallery, overlooking the proceedings, sat the five great leaders of Maritua. Pepo, the Pinnacle of the island, sat motionless on his crystalline throne, his face unreadable behind a veil of shimmering energy. Flanking him were the Sector Lords: the formidable Vega of Frostvale, her eyes as sharp and cold as glacial ice; the powerful Glint of Dravemire, his massive arms crossed over his chest; the serene Elderon of Viridawn, his presence as calm and ancient as the forest he ruled; and the gentle Lyra of Lunareth, her healing aura a faint, golden light in the solemn hall. For the first time in recorded history, they were not here to witness champions. They were here to witness children.

"The Trial of Ascent," Chancellor Caelen began, her voice cool and measured, echoing through the cavernous space, "is not a test of power, but of resonance. It measures how your soul aligns with the heart of Maritua, especially in a time of distress." She paused, her gaze sweeping across the anxious faces of the first-years. "The selection process will assess not your current abilities, but the echoes of potential that lie dormant within you. Prepare yourselves. For some, this will be a moment of triumph. For others, a revelation of limitations. And for a few... a glimpse into a future they never imagined."

A subtle tremor ran through the hall, as if the very stones were listening.

"Let the Selection begin," Caelen declared.

One by one, students were called. Each would walk to the dais, place their hand into the swirling pool of light, and wait for judgment. A clear, harmonious chime signified acceptance. A discordant, ugly clang meant rejection. The tension was agonizing. Several students were quickly dismissed, their faces falling as the sound of their failure reverberated through the silent hall.

The first of their group to be called was Nilo Thorn, the sarcastic boy from their class. He ambled up to the platform with a look of profound boredom, as if being assessed by the soul of the island was a tedious chore. He plunged his hand into the light with a theatrical sigh. For a moment, nothing happened. Then, the pool of light didn't flare or chime. Instead, it became a perfect, flawless mirror, reflecting Nilo's own unimpressed face back at him. A soft, inquisitive *boop* sound echoed, like a question being asked. The crowd murmured in confusion.

Chancellor Caelen raised an eyebrow. "Nilo Thorn," she announced, a note of surprise in her voice. "Resonance... unique. Accepted." Nilo just shrugged and walked off the dais, already looking for a place to nap.

Then came Iris's turn. She approached the platform with a determined stride, her chin high, a spark of defiance in her amber eyes. The grief of the past few days had forged a new, hard edge to her spirit. She placed her hand in the pool. It erupted in a vibrant, ferocious flare of emerald green light, and a chime rang out—clear, strong, and unwavering, with a sharp, resonant undertone of fury.

"Iris Velden," Caelen announced, a hint of admiration in her tone. "Fully Ascended." Iris gave a tight, relieved smile, her gaze finding Luca in the crowd and offering a silent message of encouragement.

Then, Zenith was called. He approached the platform with his usual unshakable composure, every movement radiating confidence and power. This was his moment, the confirmation of his destiny. He placed his hand into the swirling light. The pool exploded in a brilliant, blindingly white flare, and a pure, resonant chime began to fill the space... but then it faltered.

The light flickered. The perfect chime cracked, distorting into a sound of inner conflict. A ripple of dark, violet-tinged red, like a drop of ink in clean water, momentarily marred the surface of the pool before vanishing.

A collective gasp swept through the hall. Zenith stood frozen, his face a mask of pure shock, his jaw clenched so tight it looked like it might crack. He'd prepared for this his entire life. This... this couldn't be happening.

"Zenith Cael," Chancellor Caelen announced, her voice carefully neutral, which was somehow worse than pity. "Partially Ascended. Your resonance is... incomplete. You will be placed on provisional status."

A wave of hot, suffocating humiliation washed over Zenith. Provisional. It was a damning assessment, an implication that his potential was flawed, his spirit divided. He stepped back from the dais, his eyes darting around the hall, a flicker of raw, wounded pride crossing his features. He met Luca's gaze, and in that moment, something inside him curdled into a bitter, sharp resentment.

The list dwindled. Finally, only one name remained.

Chancellor Caelen paused, her gaze sweeping over Luca, lingering for a moment that felt like an eternity. "Luca Zarek."

Luca's heart leaped into his throat. He felt a hundred pairs of eyes on him as he walked towards the platform, his legs feeling like lead. He could hear the whispers, the snickers. *Zarek? The C-rank? This will be quick.* He reached the dais, took a shaky breath, and plunged his hand into the light.

Theworld dissolved. TheResonance Hall, the students, the leaders—it all vanished. He wasn't in the hall anymore. He was back in the Aetherfold, standing on scorched earth beneath a sky choked with ash. Before him, the five figures from his vision materialized from the gloom, their forms indistinct and terrifying. But this time, they were closer. The fifth figure, the one cloaked in shadow, its face a void, seemed to look right at him. The violet feather sigil on its back burned like a malevolent star.

A voice, vast and timeless, echoed not in his ears, but directly in his mind. It felt ancient, hungry, and horrifyingly familiar.

*"The Fold remembers. The ancient pact awakens. The balance shifts... and you, little echo... you are the keystone."*

A surge of raw, untamed power coursed through him, a feeling of being torn apart and remade, of every fear and doubt being burned away by a fire that was not his own. The

Hollowmark on his palm blazed with violet light, a light only he could see.

Back in the Resonance Hall, the pool of light erupted. It was not white or green or any other color of magic the hall had ever seen. It was a blinding, brilliant golden radiance, a color of pure, undiluted Soulstream energy. It emitted a chime so pure, so resonant, it seemed to shake the very foundations of the academy, making the stained-glass windows hum and the ancient stones vibrate with joy.

The vision shattered, and Luca found himself back on the dais, gasping for breath, sweat slicking his skin. He stumbled, catching himself on the edge of the platform, the golden light slowly receding.

The hall was utterly silent. Everyone stared, their faces a mixture of disbelief and awe.

"Luca Zarek," Chancellor Caelen announced, her voice filled with a reverence that stunned him to his core. "Fully Ascended."

He had been chosen. But for what? The weight of the vision, of the word "keystone," pressed down on him. As he turned, he saw Zenith staring at him, his face pale with shock, his eyes burning with a dark, unsettling mixture of disbelief and pure, unadulterated hatred.

As the students began to buzz with excited, confused whispers, Zenith stormed past him, his shoulder deliberately bumping Luca's. "Lucky break," he muttered, his voice low and venomous. "Don't think this makes you special." Thebitterness in his voice wasn't just disappointment. It was the sound of a bond breaking.

Luca didn't know what to say. He turned, as if to call out, but another figure caught his eye. Leaning against a far archway, half-shadowed and completely unruffled by the spectacle, stood Riven Solis. He had been watching the entire time. Their eyes met across the vast hall. Riven gave a faint, knowing nod.

"Congratulations, Zarek," he said, his voice quiet but carrying effortlessly across the space. "Looks like the Fold blinked first."

And then he pushed off the pillar and vanished into the dispersing crowd, leaving Luca alone in the center of the hall, the hero of a story he didn't understand, standing on the edge of a victory that felt terrifyingly like the beginning of a war.

## Chapter 7: The Storm Before the Ascent

"*True strength is not how you strike, but why you stand up again when you know you cannot.*"

The two days before the Trial began were a storm of a different kind. The chosen students were sequestered in the Tempest Grounds, a series of high-altitude training arenas where the very air was thin and charged with raw magic. The crystalline domes above refracted the light, bathing the floors in angular, illusory patterns. It should have felt holy. Instead, it felt like a crucible. This wasn't training; it was a desperate, frantic effort to forge children into weapons.

Hovering on silent crystal discs above the arena floor were the Academy's most formidable mentors, their expressions grim. Professor Ilaren was there, along with a stern, battle-scarred woman named Master Selix.

"Magic isn't meant to be memorized—it's meant to be *bent*!" Selix's voice cracked like a whip across the air. "If you can't command it when you're bleeding and terrified, you don't command it at all!"

Below, the elements collided. Stone pillars spun and slammed into one another. Lightning coiled around collapsing wind tunnels. Flame surged beneath glyph-mazes that rearranged themselves with cruel speed. Magic was not color and flash here. It was breath, blood, and grit.

In the eye of the chaos, Zenith Cael moved like a war-born symphony. His earlier failure in the Resonance Hall had not broken him; it had filled him with a cold, terrifying fire. A barrier of solid light surged up in front of him—he shattered it with a concussive pulse of raw force. Three elemental training dummies attacked in sequence—he redirected their spells, chained his own, and launched a sonic burst that blasted them to dust without even seeming to break a sweat. He didn't flinch. He didn't smirk. But his every gesture radiated a clear, defiant message: *I belong here. I am better than this. I will not fail again.*

Theother students couldn't help but watch, mesmerized by his power. Until the crash.

"ZAREK!"

Theshout came too late. Luca had misfired. Again. His fire rune had fizzled, shorted, and belched a cloud of foul-smelling smoke. He'd tried to follow it with a wind glyph to disperse the smoke, but his spell snapped mid-spin, and his own momentum carried him—hard—into a floating obsidian rune-column. The column, designed to test defensive shields, tottered for a moment, then fell with him.

The arena *shook*. There was a stunned pause, followed by a ripple of laughter.

Zenith turned, his arms folded, a cruel smirk finally touching his lips. "Planning to master pratfall magic instead, Zarek? Perhaps you can trip your opponents to death."

Luca coughed, sitting up in a cloud of swirling smoke and dust. His pride hurt far more than his bruised ribs. He saw a few students covering their mouths to hide their grins.

Only one face remained still. Iris. She stood near the far ring, her hands woven into a complex mimicry loop. Her training was different from Zenith's brute force. It was elegant, reactive, a dance of redirection. She weaved through enemy spells, catching them, twisting them, and turning their own force against them without resistance. Her body moved like water, her aura shimmering like dusk. But even from across the arena, Luca could see the crack under her control. In one spar, her redirected flame spell overtook its target far too quickly. The training dummy didn't just deactivate; it combusted, its metal frame melting in a flash of intense heat. Her jaw tensed, and she took a sharp breath, like someone dragging a painful memory from a locked chest. Her power was growing, but her grief was making it dangerously unstable.

That night, sleep didn't come for Luca. It broke him open. He was pulled back into the Aetherfold, but this time, there was no gentle greeting. He found himself standing on a vast, frozen lake under a sky veined with tearing, violet light.

From a rift in the sky, Elarion descended. But this was not the patient keeper Luca had met before. His robes were darker, and his face was shadowed beneath a hood that seemed to drink the light. He was no longer a guide; he was a master.

He raised a hand, and the world obeyed.

The frozen lake shattered, hurling Luca into a desert storm of lightning and fire. There were no rules here, no safety. Every spell Luca tried to cast was stolen from him, twisted by the Fold's reality and turned back against him. He tried to summon a shield—it became a cage of burning light that seared his skin. He tried to cast fire—it rebounded and scorched his leg.

He fought shadows, twisted versions of himself, colder and perfected. *"You are just a child pretending to matter,"* one of them whispered as it drove him to his knees. He bled. He broke. But he didn't scream. Not once did Elarion help. He only watched—from the cliffs of a dream, from the heart of a dust devil, from inside the eyes of the illusions that beat him down. He was not instructing. He was observing. Testing.

Then came the beast. It was a towering, nightmarish creature with smoke-black skin, six burning eyes, and a tail made of chittering, razor-sharp blades. Luca struck it with flame—it only grew stronger, absorbing the heat. He tried ice—it roared and shattered the ground. He was crushed under its weight, his ribs screaming in protest, his heart hammering with a terror so profound it threatened to swallow him whole. He tried to move, but his legs felt like glass.

*"You're just a child pretending to matter,"* the shade whispered again, its voice his own.

Luca closed his eyes, his body broken, his magic useless. He was going to fail. He was going to be consumed. And in the darkness, a memory surfaced. His mother, her hands gentle but firm, shielding him from a storm when he was a boy. Her words, soft but sharp as steel: *"Real strength isn't about how you strike, Luca. It's about why you stand up again when you know you cannot."*

His fingers twitched. The pain hadn't left. But something inside him shifted. In that moment of absolute surrender, something screamed louder than his fear. It wasn't his magic. It was his *will.*

He stopped trying to cast. He stopped trying to fight. He just *felt.*

He felt the storm. He felt the rhythm of the false world. He felt the current of the Fold that pulsed under it all, the same current he'd felt from the island. He raised a hand—not with force, but with a quiet, resonant understanding.

And the air *bent* to his will.

Lightning coiled from the heavens, not summoned by a spell, but *called* by his attunement. It didn't strike. It waited. It *listened.*

The beast lunged, its six eyes burning with malice. Luca whispered—not a word of power, but a single, pure frequency, a note of absolute balance that he pulled from the heart of the Fold itself.

The beast *froze* mid-lunge. Then, with a sound like a thousand shattering mirrors, it burst into a shower of violet glass.

Everything went quiet. The wind calmed. The firestorm died.

Elarion stepped forward, no longer a shadow, but the serene keeper once more. He didn't offer praise. He simply placed his palm over Luca's heart. A sigil of pure, white light burned there for a moment—it hurt, a deep, soul-aching pain, but it felt earned.

"You have unlocked the current," Elarion said, his voice low and final. "You do not command the storm. You have become its eye. When the real trial comes... you will bleed again. But this time, you will remember how to rise."

Luca's legs finally gave out. He collapsed, drifting into the dream's closing silence. But as his consciousness faded, he smiled. Not because he had won. Not because he was strong.

But because, for the first time, he had stood up without knowing if he could. And the world had answered.

# Chapter 8: Let the Arena Decide

"G*lory is not a gift. It is a debt, paid for on the edge of grief.*"

The morning of the Trial of Ascent arrived not with a sunrise, but with a sound. It was a deep, grinding hum that resonated from high above Nebula, the sound of a celestial lock coming undone. High in the sky, the Crucible Halo, a colossal, rotating ring of ancient stone and pulsating glyphs, began to stir. For centuries, it had remained dormant, a silent crown on the sky. Now, it rotated slowly, its massive sections aligning with a terrifying, final purpose. It was not a crown; it was an executioner's block.

Down below, the chosen students gathered in the antechamber, the air thick with the metallic taste of fear. The mood was not celebratory. It was funereal. Every footstep on the cold stone floor echoed louder than it should have. Luca could feel the pulse of the great arena above them, a living, watching presence that seemed to lick its lips in anticipation. Some students murmured quiet prayers. Others stared ahead, their faces pale masks of resolve. But most eyes flicked upward, toward the ancient arena floating like a celestial engine, grinding to full power.

"Those bruises—" A familiar voice beside him, low but sharp. Iris. She had made her way through the line of nervous students, her amber eyes fixed on the faint, discolored marks visible on Luca's side beneath his uniform, remnants of his phantom battle in the Aetherfold. "Did you fall down the stairs again, or...?" He managed a faint, wry smirk. "Just a dream."

Her brow furrowed. "That was from a *dream*?"

He winced as he shifted his weight. "It didn't like me either."

Up in the high skybox, Pepo sat still as a statue, encased in the silent, shimmering crystal of his viewing chamber. Beside him, the four Sector Lords were figures of grim solemnity. They had seen too many trials, too many champions rise and fall. They knew this day was different.

A deep chime rang, and a voice, magically amplified to the power of a god's, boomed across the assembled realms. It was Master Selix, her voice a verdict carved in stone.

"By decree of Nebula Academia, under the watchful eyes of the Council of the Five Sector Lords, and in accordance with the ancient pacts—the Trial of Ascent shall now commence!" she declared. "All matches will be witnessed, overseen, and bound under the Trial Accord. Let these laws be known: No killing. No lethal magic. Knockout or surrender shall mark the victor. Intent to maim shall be punished by immediate expulsion. Once a match begins, there are no second chances. Victory will not belong to the strongest... but to those who endure."

Above the arena, the glyph-bound rings of the Crucible Halo ignited with a brilliant blue fire. The first names were called.

"Match One: Luca Zarek of Nebula... versus Tharos Venn of Frostvale."

A hush fell. Luca's blood ran cold. He took a shaky breath and stepped forward onto the teleportation glyph. The world dissolved in a shimmer of light, and he reappeared in the center of the vast, floating arena. Across from him stood Tharos Venn, a boy who looked less sculpted from flesh and more forged from iron and ice. Bands of shimmering metal coiled around his arms like frozen vipers, glowing faintly with contained power. He didn't nod. He didn't smile. He just raised a hand.

The match began. Tharos struck first. Threads of molten metal, superheated but moving with the speed of whips, lashed through the air. Luca dodged left, then right, sparks searing his sleeves. He tried to summon his magic, to form the shields he'd practiced, but the sheer pressure of the arena, the thousands of watching eyes, the memory of his own inadequacy—it all came crashing down. His will, the key to his magic, crumbled. His wind glyph misfired into a weak puff of air. His fire rune hissed and died with a pathetic fizzle. He was back to being the helpless boy from the training yard.

He spun, desperately trying a simple burst rune—and it backfired, detonating with a dull thud that knocked him flat onto the shifting arena stone. The air left his lungs in a painful gasp. A groan of disappointment rippled from the crowd. Then, a coil of steel, no longer molten but cold and hard, wrapped around his ankle like a hungry snake, and Tharos yanked.

Luca was dragged across the stone floor like a ragdoll, his head slamming against the ground hard enough to rattle his teeth. The coil hissed as it began to tighten, ready to crush. And then... a searing warmth blossomed in his right palm, right where the invisible Hollowmark was etched into his soul. It pulsed, once, a vibrant and aware beat of violet energy that no one else could see.

No one, except one. High above, Pepo, the Pinnacle of Maritua, stirred. He leaned forward slightly in his crystalline throne, his eyes narrowed. A single, whispered name escaped his lips, a sound so quiet it was lost in the roar of the crowd. "...Elarion." But it was too late. Luca, defeated and humiliated, was escorted from the arena.

The next phase was announced: Tag Matches. Luca stood beside Iris in the shadow of the next battlefield platform, his breath shallow, the bruise on his ribs feeling like it had its own heartbeat.

"Okay," Luca muttered, his voice shaking slightly. "New plan. You win. I... try not to get turned into a puddle. We both go home."

"Didn't know we had a 'go home' clause," Iris replied, tying her braid tighter, her expression fierce and focused.

"I may have invented it."

"Relax," she said, her voice dipping softer now, sensing his terror. "You're not alone this time. Just react. Don't overthink."

Before he could answer, the announcer cried, "Match Two: Iris Velden and Luca Zarek of Nebula... versus Renya Vale and Crinn of Lunareth."

Thearena shifted, platforms of stone and mist rotating into place. Their opponents appeared. Renya Vale was a shimmering enigma, while her partner, Crinn, was a quiet, grey-eyed boy holding twin psiblades that flickered like solidified illusions. Then, without warning, Renya split. Five identical versions of her blinked into existence, all moving in different directions. Crinn charged forward, his blades raised, one trailing sparks, the other trailing shadows.

Luca blinked. "Okay, no one mentioned the 'five clones plus knives' situation—" A psiblade grazed his shoulder. A burning cold sliced through his nerves. He grunted, stumbling back, but he didn't fall. He was about to panic, to freeze up just as he had before. But then, from the sidelines, a voice scoffed, loud enough to carry over the hum of the arena.

"Should have sent someone else with Iris. Zarek's just dead weight."

It hit him harder than the blade. The laughter. The whispers. The confirmation of every fear his dream-self had thrown at him. He was going to fail her. He closed his eyes, shame and fear a rising tide threatening to swallow him whole.

And in that darkness, a voice. Elarion's. *"You think fear is your weakness. But it is the only part of you that does not lie. Cast when the world screams. Cast when your fear tries to swallow you. That is when the Fold watches."*

He opened his eyes. His pulse slowed. He stopped trying to remember glyphs. He stopped trying to force his magic. He just... listened. He listened to the hum of the arena, the crackle of the psiblades, the frantic beat of his own heart. And he felt the current.

His hand moved, not in a spell-form, but in an instinctive, intuitive gesture. A warmth, ancient and undeniable, pulsed from the Hollowmark, up his arm, and into his very soul. A crack of compressed thunder, tinged with a faint violet light, burst from his palm. A radial glyph, the same feather sigil from the stone, snapped into existence mid-air. It didn't shoot lightning. It unleashed a wave of pure, disruptive resonance.

The five echo-forms of Renya flickered—and the real one staggered, clutching her head as her illusion shattered. The crowd gasped.

Iris, seeing her opening, moved. Crinn, his psiblade flickering back into his hand, was met with a whirlwind of controlled fury. Iris danced through his attacks, her hands weaving a mimicry arc that caught his blade, pulled it through an entropy fold, and hurled it back at him, shattering his own defensive glyph. He dropped, unconscious. It was over.

The crowd roared, this time in approval. Iris landed beside Luca, cheeks flushed, hair wild. "I think," he said, breathing hard, "I like your bad side."

She smirked. "Then you're lucky it's always forward-facing."

Their victory was followed by Nilo Thorn's match. Paired with a nervous but capable mage named Alistair, Nilo faced two hulking brutes from Dravemire. As they charged, roaring, Alistair began to form a complex defensive barrier. Nilo, however, simply yawned and, with a lazy flick of his wrist, conjured a small, perfectly formed mirror glyph. The Dravemire duo's own spell, a volley of sharp rock shards, hit the mirror and shot back at them with twice the speed. They yelped, stumbling over each other in a comical clatter of armor.

"Oops," Nilo muttered, a faint smirk on his lips. "Guess you should really *reflect* on your choices."

Finally, the announcer's voice boomed again. "Match Four: Zenith Cael and his partner, Seraphina Bellweather of Nebula... versus the Mistbinders of Viridawn!"

Zenith stepped forward alone, his support mage, a shy girl with freckles, scrambling to keep up. He didn't even look at her. His fists were clenched, his jaw tight. He was a storm of cold fury, desperate to erase the shame of his 'incomplete' resonance. Across the field stood Eira and Solen Armath, twin conjurers from Viridawn. In perfect unison, they raised their arms, and a thick, disorienting fog blossomed across the arena.

Zenith didn't wait. He launched himself forward, a cannon of pure fire and force. He shattered their first wave of smoke-wolf illusions with a volatile, spiraling arc of flame. The crowd cheered his power. But he was reckless. He overextended, leaving his partner unprotected. As he landed from a fiery leap, the real spectral beasts, two panthers made of mist and shadow, pounced on her. She raised a barrier, but it was too late. It shattered like glass, and she fell with a scream.

"Useless!" Zenith shouted, his voice cracking with a rage that was aimed as much at himself as at her. He turned to face the Mistbinders again, but now they were closer, their movements perfectly synchronized, their spells a web of disorientation and misdirection. He was powerful, but he was one person against a perfectly coordinated team.

They overwhelmed him. A lattice of hardened fog crystallized around him, and a spectral panther sank its cold, magical fangs into his shoulder, sending him crashing to the stone floor. His flames snuffed out, his breath torn from his chest. He was defeated.

As he lay there, his vision blurring, the humiliation a thousand times worse than Luca's, he saw Luca and Iris in the stands, watching. He, the prodigy, had failed, while Zarek, the C-rank failure, had found a way to win. The injustice of it, the sheer wrongness, was a poison in his soul.

And in the silence of his defeat, the air in the arena *curled.* The clouds churning above didn't just darken; they seemed to thin, to become brittle. A low hum began to rise—not from the earth, not from the air—but from *beneath the silence* itself.

Then—one sound. A single, distant thunderclap that was not thunder. It was not a storm.

It was a knock. From the other side of the world. And the sky... the sky forgot how to breathe.

# Chapter 9: The Day Memory Bled

"*The most terrifying monsters are not the ones that hunt us in the dark. They are the ones we once loved.*"

The knock had come. And something, ancient and malevolent, answered.

The world had gone still. Not silent—it was *held*. Every breath in the Crucible caught, every sound swallowed by an oppressive, unnatural vacuum that descended upon the arena. Above Nebula, the clouds didn't just part; they *split* with a soundless, tearing violence. A jagged, violet-black rift, like a fresh wound in the very fabric of reality, tore open in the sky. It pulsed with a silence older than sound, a void that drank the light and cast a shadow that seemed to drain the color from the world below.

And from its depths... he descended. He did not fall, nor did he fly. He *unfolded*—like a nightmare too long kept in a dark corner of the mind, now unfurling its impossible, grotesque shape into the waking world.

His robes were not woven fabric, but layers of articulated, polished bone, fused as if they'd been grown directly onto his skeletal form. His face was partially obscured by a mask made from a shattered skull, carved with symbols that no human mouth dared speak. Only his thin, bloodless lips moved. His voice didn't just speak; it slithered through the bones of the arena, a memory of a forgotten truth whispered directly into the minds of all who heard it, chilling them to their very soul.

"By the Pact of the Pale Flame," the figure intoned, his voice resonating with ancient, forbidden power, "we, the Sorcerers of Viralith, do break the Accord of Silence."

The name *Viralith* meant nothing to the students. But in the high gallery, the world ended. Pepo lurched forward, his hands clenching on his crystalline throne with a sharp *click*. Vega's face went ashen. Glint's knuckles turned white. A sacred vow, laid down by the island's founders, had just been shattered like glass. The island's darkest secret was no longer buried.

The skeletal figure smiled, a predator's grin that promised only agony. "I am Lazherak," he declared, his voice a bone-deep proclamation. "Bonechant Whisperer of the Pale Flame. Let the dead remember us."

Then, from the rift, they manifested. And the true horror began.

They were not mere shadows or summoned beasts. They were students. Names whispered in corridors. Faces etched into dorm walls and fading yearbooks. Their bodies were twisted, warped by a power that defied rest, flesh clinging where it shouldn't, bones jutting through their tattered academy uniforms like thorns through silk. Their eyes did not glow; they pulsed with violet wounds, leaking dark energy. Lazherak hadn't summoned soldiers. He had unearthed tragedies. Maritua's fallen—ripped from their rest and reborn as warnings.

And Iris saw her. Floating in silence, her movements an eerie, macabre dance of grace. Kaelin.

Her cracked silver pendant, the twin to the one Iris now clutched at her own throat, still dangled from her neck. But her eyes were hollowed stars, glassy and distant, reflecting nothing but the void. A cold entropy shimmered around her fingertips like leaking stardust.

Iris's world, which had been gray with grief, shattered into a million points of agony. A sound, a choked, disbelieving sob, tore from her throat.

Chaos erupted. The Sector Lords, their faces masks of grim fury, leaped into battle. Vega became a swirling vortex of ice, hurling colossal shards at the corrupted. Glint burst from the ground in a storm of living metal, weaving colossal shields. Elderon slammed his staff to the earth, and a forest of thorned roots erupted, impaling the desecrated forms.

But it wasn't enough. The corrupted students fought with an unnatural strength, their cursed magic feeding on the pure energy of the Lords. For every one they struck down, two more took its place.

"Kaelin..." Iris whispered, her voice breaking. She ran. No hesitation. No fear. Only a desperate, world-ending need to reach her friend. She ran toward the face she had once braided flowers with, the voice that had once laughed at her jokes. "Kaelin, it's me! It's Iris! Remember?"

Kaelin's head twitched. The hollow eyes focused on her. And then, entropy flared. A wave of pure, unmaking energy blasted from Kaelin's fingertips.

"Iris, no—!" Luca screamed, but he was too late. The blast threw Iris backwards like a ragdoll. She hit a stone wall with a sickening thud and crumpled to the ground, her vision swimming.

Then, from above, something fell. Fast. Silent. A blur cloaked in dusk and fury. Riven.

He landed without a sound, his black coat swirling around him. The blue flame on his shoulder pulsed with a living light. He carried a sword, its blade thin as a whisper, humming with suppressed, ancient power.

Lazherak snapped, "A child playing hero! Still you persist, Last Ash!"

Riven didn't reply. His blade did. He *moved*, and time itself seemed to stutter. Blue-gold slivers, chrono-flickers, danced in his wake. He didn't run around his enemies; he seemed to step *between* the moments, appearing and disappearing in the blink of an eye. A corrupted student lunged—Riven walked *through* it, his blade tracing a line in the air. The corpse didn't fall apart; it was simply *undone*, collapsing into a pile of dust and bone as if its place in time had been erased.

But Lazherak only laughed. "You are but a flicker against the tide." He raised his arms, and the ground trembled. A new shape rose from the blood-soaked stone. It was fifteen feet tall, plated in glistening, black chitin, its limbs bound with screaming, red chains. Its jaw hung open in a gaping maw of nothingness. This was the Grave-Titan, a monstrosity born of a thousand sorrows.

The Titan attacked. Riven met its crushing blow, and the impact rattled the entire arena. He was fast, impossibly fast, but the Titan was an anchor of despair in the flow of time. It was too strong. Its chains lashed out, catching Riven's blade, locking it. The creature kicked, and Riven was thrown, slamming into a shattered pillar, his coat ripped, a line of blood tracing his lip. He rose—limping, his breath ragged—but he was losing. The Grave-Titan roared and lunged again. The blow connected. Riven flew, hit the ground, and lay still.

All hope seemed to die with him. The Sector Lords were battered and bleeding. The students were cowering. The arena was a graveyard.

And Kaelin, her movements silent and graceful, drifted towards the fallen Iris.

Iris, her body screaming in pain, clawed at the ground, trying to crawl away, but her strength was gone. She looked up into the hollow, empty eyes of her best friend. Sobbing soundlessly, her hands trembling, she pulled the memory-locket from her neck and held it out. "Please, Kaelin," she wept, her voice raw. "Remember us... Remember me..."

The pendant touched Kaelin's chest. The corrupted form froze. Kaelin's head tilted, and for one, impossible, heartbreaking heartbeat, a flicker of recognition sparked in the void of her eyes. A real smile, small and crooked, touched her lips.

"...Iris," she breathed, her voice a fragile whisper, a ghost of a sound. "...Sing our song... I'm... cold..."

And then the light went out. The warmth drained from her form so quickly it was like touching winter itself. Iris broke. A soundless scream ripped through her as Kaelin's body dissolved in her arms, not falling, but disintegrating into a soft, slow cascade of gray ash that clung to Iris's trembling hands.

"She was meant to stand beside you in the flames of tomorrow," Lazherak howled, a triumphant, mad sound. "Instead... she becomes your first offering!"

As the last of Kaelin's ash settled, the very ground of the Crucible groaned. A thin, violet fracture spread from where she had fallen, weaving through the ruined arena like a crack in a mirror. The ancient seals, long dormant beneath the stone, began to pulse with a dark, forbidden light.

Lazherak turned his gaze to the sky, his smile widening in chilling, ecstatic anticipation. Something was coming. Not from his rift. But from below.

"Let him come," he whispered, his voice a chilling invitation. "Let the great mistake of stillness descend to meet his ruin."

Above Nebula, the sky *shattered*. A blinding streak of silver and crimson tore through the heavens, not lightning, but a falling star trailing ancient sigils that burned themselves onto the air. A presence, vast and undeniable, plummeted towards the ravaged Crucible, a force of nature promising a reckoning. And the entire island held its breath.

# Chapter 10: The Red Phantom and the Aftermath

"*In the face of true chaos, order is the most terrifying weapon of all.*"

The sky above the ravaged Crucible did not just hold a rift; it held a judgment. The blinding streak of silver and crimson that had shattered the heavens was not lightning, nor was it a spell. It was a presence, a force of nature descending with the speed of a falling star, and it brought with it a silence more profound than the preceding chaos. As it descended, the frantic screams, the crackle of dying magic, and the panicked whispers were all extinguished, replaced by an unnerving, absolute calm.

He did not land. He simply *arrived*. He stood in the center of the carnage, a figure cloaked in a red so deep it seemed to absorb the very light around it. The cloak billowed with an unnatural weight, rippling like a river of condensed night. His form was humanoid, but he wore a smooth, featureless mask of polished white bone, devoid of any expression save for two glowing, crimson eye-slits that held the cold, steady intensity of distant stars.

The stunned silence of the spectators broke into a wave of hushed, awestruck whispers that spread through the stands like wildfire.

"It can't be..."

"The legends are true..."

"The Red Phantom..."

He was a myth, a bedtime story told to frighten children into behaving. He was Pepo's personal guardian, the Royal Guardian, a being said to be as ancient as the island itself, a relic of a forgotten age of warfare.

Lazherak, the necromancer, his skeletal face still etched with a mad grin, watched the Phantom's arrival with dark, triumphant glee. He extended a skeletal hand, a gesture of perverse welcome. "So, the great mistake of stillness finally shows itself," he hissed, his voice slithering into every mind. "Pepo's chained dog, let off its leash at last! You are too late, relic! Your time is over!"

The Phantom didn't speak. His presence was the only pronouncement necessary. He raised one hand, palm open. A quiet pulse of crimson energy blew outward—not a destructive surge, but a gentle, absolute *correction* to the violated space, a wave of pure order that pushed back Lazherak's chaotic, deathly aura.

The Grave-Titan, the fifteen-foot corpse hulking and veined with glowing green runes, lumbered forward, its bones creaking like ancient trees. It roared, a sound like a hundred tombs groaning open, a voice meant to tear the soul from the body. It charged, stone cracking beneath its feet.

The Phantom, in response, simply raised one hand again. Calm. Effortless. A burst of pure, concentrated kinetic force—not fire, not lightning, but reality-twisting pressure—erupted from his palm. It struck the Grave-Titan mid-charge, launching the colossal beast as if it were a child's toy. It slammed into the upper arena wall with a shockwave that pulverized entire rows of spectator seating, raining crystal shards down on the battlefield below.

The monster, impossibly, stood again. It howled in rage and swung a massive, bone-cracking fist. The Phantom, with a speed that defied physics, caught the blow with one hand. Dust and debris spiraled out from the impact. Then, he twisted. A glowing, spiraling sigil of pure, crushing power erupted from his grip, not just stopping the arm, but *unmaking* it. The Titan's arm disintegrated, its bones scattering like splintered wood.

Before the creature could even register its own agony, the Phantom struck again. He stomped once on the stone floor. A glowing red ring, a sealing sigil, etched itself into the ground beneath the Grave-Titan. The colossal corpse didn't fall; it crumpled inward, its form compressing with a sickening crunch until it was nothing more than a faint, swirling vortex of dark particles, which the wind then scattered to nothing.

Across the ruins, Vega struggled to her feet, frostblades in hand, her eyes wide with a mixture of awe and terror. "What... what was that strike?"

Glint staggered out from behind a shattered wall, molten metal still dripping from a grievous wound in his arm. "He didn't strike with force," he muttered, his voice raspy. "He struck with *finality*."

Elderon simply watched, his bark-covered arm trembling, the life-giving green energy within it flickering low. "The land itself remembers him," he breathed.

"You..." Lazherak growled, his madness tipping into pure, venomous hatred. "You were bound by the old laws, but never truly gone! If you wish for balance, you will drown in imbalance!" He raised both arms, his bone-chains rattling, and the earth itself split. A veritable sea of the dead, ten thousand skeletal corpses, rose in a chittering, clattering wave, clambering over each other, their eye sockets glowing with a dim, malevolent light.

The tide of bone and death surged forward. But the heroes of Maritua, though battered and bleeding, were not yet broken.

"He needs time!" Vega roared, seeing the Phantom begin to draw slow, deliberate crimson rings of power from the air into his own body, charging a spell of immense scale. She gritted her teeth and summoned a rising glacier wall, slowing the flood with groaning, cracking ice. Glint roared in defiance and forged a spiraling disc of razor-sharp metal that spun like a cyclone through the masses, shattering bone but dulling quickly under the sheer numbers.

Zenith, his face a mask of fury and despair, stood his ground. He roared, a sound of pure, unadulterated rage, and began chanting, his magic flaring, now twisted with a dark shimmer of his own wounded pride. He sent wild, uncontrolled bursts of flame into the unending tide, incinerating dozens at a time.

Iris, her body screaming with pain, pushed herself up. The soundless sob she had suppressed for Kaelin now manifested as a cold, burning fury that pulsed through her veins. Her magic, usually flowing and precise, became a whip of concentrated, vengeful memory. She lashed out, twisting the corrupted energy of the approaching corpses, forcing them to turn on each other in a grotesque whirlwind of self-destruction.

Luca, seeing his friends making their desperate last stand, staggered forward. The Hollowmark on his palm pulsed with a searing heat. He ignored the pain, ignored his exhaustion, and thrust out his hand—not trying to cast a spell, but simply *attuning* to the raw chaos. A wave of disruptive violet energy pulsed from him, not strong enough to destroy, but enough to *unbalance.* Corrupted forms stumbled, their eerie, synchronized movements stuttering, giving the Sector Lords a precious moment of reprieve.

And from a pile of shattered rubble, Nilo Thorn emerged, dusting off his uniform with an exasperated sigh. "Oh, *fine*," he muttered to himself. "I suppose my lunch break is officially canceled." He launched into the fray, not with raw power, but with infuriating cleverness. He created phantom illusions of dancing grilled cheese sandwiches, drawing masses of the bone-horde into comical, confused circles. He deployed bubbles of absolute silence around necromantic commanders, breaking their chain of command and turning entire battalions into a tripping, stumbling mess.

It was absurd. But it was working. It was buying the Phantom the seconds he needed.

His charging complete, his crimson glow now blinding, the Red Phantom slammed his palms together.

**BOOM.**

A wave of red energy exploded outward—thunderless, soundless, but absolute. It tore through the remaining undead army like wind through paper. Bones turned to dust. Skulls cracked in mid-roar. Swords clattered to the ground as their wielders vanished into nothingness. In seconds, the army was gone. Erased.

Only Lazherak remained, his robes flaring, his eyes full of furious, impossible hatred. He snarled, knowing he was beaten.

With a final curse, he flung a handful of shimmering black dust, creating a blinding, corrosive cloud. As the Phantom's power pushed through the darkness, Lazherak dissolved into a whirl of boneflies and black ash, retreating into the shadows from whence he came.

Silence. The Crucible was a grave. The battle was over. The ground was stained crimson, a testament to the battle's brutal cost.

And then, she arrived. Her coming was not heralded by a thunderclap or a flash of light, but by a sudden, profound quiet in the heart of the chaos. She walked through the smoke and ash as if it parted for her alone, a serene presence in a world torn by violence. Lyra of Lunareth.. Her cloak shimmered with threads of woven light, and her long, golden braid glowed with a soft, steady warmth. She moved barefoot across the blackened, blood-slick stones, and where her hands passed, the impossible happened. Wounds closed. Broken bones rewove themselves. Students who'd been crushed beneath rubble now breathed in gasps of astonishment, pain receding like a dream. Vega's frost-burns faded. Glint's armor resealed itself. Even Riven, still unconscious, groaned as his cracked ribs snapped back into place. Her healing was her language, and it was the most powerful Maritua had ever seen.

As the last of the wounded was tended to, a new sound arose: the angry, fearful roar of the crowd. Questions rippled through the stands, turning into a dangerous unease.

Pepo, his face grim, raised one hand. His voice, amplified by ancient magic, resonated throughout Nebula. "By my authority, as the Head of Maritua, and by the Accord of Silence now shattered—I summon the Emergency Council of Core!"

He turned his gaze to the heroes. "Luca Zarek. Iris Velden. Riven Solis. Report to the Head's Sanctum. Immediately."

Luca nodded, still dazed. As he, Iris, and a now-conscious Riven began to move, Iris's eyes darted around, searching. Her face, already pale, lost its remaining color.

"Wait," she said, her voice laced with a growing panic. "Where's Zenith?"

No one had an answer. No one had seen when he'd vanished. He had been there, fighting with a desperate fury near the edge of the ruins. And then... he was gone.

# Chapter 11: The Fold of Broken Memory

"*History is not a story told, but a wound that is remembered.*"

The Head's Sanctum, hours after the Crucible's chaos, felt colder than the night outside. The air, usually humming with Maritua's ambient magic, was thick with unspoken questions and the heavy silence of grief. Pepo stood before a shimmering holographic map of Maritua, his crimson robe a stark slash of color against the cool blue light. Lyra, Riven, Luca, and a frantic Iris stood before him.

"His energy signature... it just vanished," Lyra whispered, her voice softer than breath, yet heavier than any scream. "There was a flicker—a dark, cold aura—where he was last seen, but it was fleeting. Like a shadow stepping through a door no one else could see. He's... not here."

Before anyone could respond, the Sanctum's primary surveillance orb, a floating sphere of crystal and light, sputtered to life with a distorted hum. Broken images flickered across its surface—static, smoke, and shattered stone—before settling on a single, frozen frame.

It was Zenith. He was standing alone, not in the ruined arena, but deep below the academy, in a dark, forgotten hallway carved from ancient, weeping stone, lit by the pale, dying light of decaying glyphs. Above an archway behind him, a single number burned faintly into the rock: **300.**

Then, the image warped, and Zenith's face filled the screen. He was pale, his eyes distant, as if he were staring through the orb and into a place far, far away. From the static, a chorus of ghostly voices rose, not one, not many, but something in between, a layered whisper that seemed to come from the stones themselves.

*"Zenith."*

The chamber froze. Iris stumbled back, a hand flying to her mouth. Luca's pulse hammered against his ribs like a war drum. Then the feed cut to black.

"Floor 300," Pepo said, his voice grim. "A sealed sub-level. A place of quarantine. Its true purpose was lost to time, part of the Accord of Silence." He turned, his gaze settling with an immense weight on Luca. "But now I see. It is not just a prison. It is a gateway. A weak point in the Veil."

Orion, the master of the Grand Archive, appeared as a shimmering hologram beside Pepo. "Zenith's disappearance was not a random abduction," he explained, his voice grave. "His bitterness, his wounded pride after the Selection, the dark shimmer in his magic—they made him a target. He resonated with the Fold's corrupted energy. In his despair, he unknowingly sought a place that would accept his pain, and the island, in its own wounded state, showed him the way."

Iris gasped, her eyes wide with fresh understanding and renewed terror. She clutched Luca's coat, her knuckles white. "Don't get lost in there, Luca," she pleaded, her voice a ragged whisper. "Don't you dare. Just... find him. Please."

Luca met her gaze, his own resolve hardening into steel. "I will find him, Iris. I promise."

Pepo stepped forward. "TheFold is not a place, Luca, but a dimension of living memory. It feeds on what is hidden. To lose yourself there is to become another forgotten echo. We believe your unique resonance, the Hollowmark, is the only way to navigate it. It is the key."

Riven, silent until now, spoke, his voice low and certain. "You can't fight a memory, Luca. You have to endure it. Let it wash over you, but do not let it drown you."

Luca nodded, understanding. He lay on a cot as a red-sand sigil was drawn on the floor, the ancient ritual to open the way. The sigil pulsed once, twice—then unraveled like torn fabric, spilling a tangible darkness into the room. He closed his eyes, thinking of Iris's plea, of Riven's advice, of Zenith's haunted face. The world tilted, and he fell—not down, but inward.

He awoke in the Aetherfold. Elarion stood before him, a somber, spectral guide in a landscape of churning, chaotic memory.

"Awake, Keystone," Elarion's voice echoed. "You are not here by accident. To find the one you seek, you must first understand the wound he has fallen into. You must witness the memory of Maritua's own breaking."

The dreamscape around them fractured, reforming into a vast, cosmic canvas. "Observe, Luca," Elarion said. "The true beginning."

Holographic fragments of history flickered into existence. Luca saw a vision of Earth in the year

**2037**, a world of towering, futuristic cities. He then saw a cataclysm, a wave of energy that did not destroy the island of Mauritius, but transformed it, imbuing it with a sentient, magical consciousness. The new, living island, Maritua, rejected the invasive technologies of its past, growing its own defenses, its own balance. At its heart rose Nebula, not just a capital, but a self-sustaining marvel, the tallest and largest structure on the island, a living part of its consciousness.

"But balance is fragile," Elarion's voice resonated, now tinged with sorrow. "And some seek to shatter it for their own twisted ideals."

A new vision formed: a dark, oppressive underground lab. A younger Viralith appeared, his eyes burning with a desperate, brilliant light. He was not a monster. He was a dreamer.th

"Viralith was a true prodigy of Maritua's first era," Elarion said softly. "But even the brightest flame can warp when pressed by grief. He lost his family, his students, his entire village to a magical catastrophe no one could control. That pain carved him hollow." Luca watched as Viralith knelt in the ashes of his home, a scorched child's toy lying beside him, his hands pressed to the dead earth as if begging it to give back what it had taken.

"He believed Maritua's magic was cruelly chaotic," Elarion continued. "He dreamed of a world where memories—every love, every joy—would never be lost. He sought not immortality of flesh, but of meaning. His partners, including the ambitious Lazherak, believed in him, for they too were broken by loss. But in their desperation to control life and death, they went too far. Lazherak twisted Viralith's work, and the first corrupted echoes were born. United in their grief and desperate ambition, Viralith and his followers made a forbidden vow, an agreement to shatter the natural cycle of life and loss. They would achieve a perfect, unchanging world by binding memories to the physical realm, no matter the cost.

**This was the Pact of the Pale Flame.** The consequences were catastrophic. Their ritual tore a hole in reality, and the attempt to preserve memory became a war against it, with the sky bleeding light and memories being torn from the living.

"Facing total annihilation," Elarion narrated, "Pepo's predecessors sealed Viralith and his order away within the Fold itself. This was the Accord of Silence, a solemn vow to erase their names from history, hoping to sever the roots of their corrupted power. But a prophecy was given: that one day, when the seals weakened, five new legends would stand between Maritua and its end."

Elarion gestured, and images of Luca, Iris, Riven, and Nilo appeared, glowing softly. "You were chosen not for what you are, but for what you can become. But the fifth legend," Elarion said, and he gestured not to a clear image, but to a swirling vortex of chaotic, colorful light that refused to take a solid form. "The fifth cannot be contained by a single image, for it is a being of pure possibility. It is not human. It is the island's unbound soul, its final, wild protector. The ancient texts call it the Anomaly, a bug in the perfect code of creation. But there is a simpler name for this beautiful, chaotic imperfection, one whispered in the deepest corners of our history. We call it **Glitch**."

Elarion's gaze became intense. "You do not *find* such a being. You must prove yourselves worthy of its attention. It will awaken only when the island's despair is deepest, when a sacrifice of perfect order is made to call forth its perfect chaos. Only then will it choose to appear."

He let the weight of that sink in before adding softly, "The prophecy speaks of these five. But remember, Luca... a prophecy is a map, not a cage. It does not account for the hero who is not chosen, but who chooses to rise from his own ashes."

The vision faded, leaving only Luca and Elarion in the white void. "The dream's purpose is a trial, to awaken your true potential," Elarion stated firmly. "The Hollowmark on your palm is not a curse. It is a key. It links you to the very despair that has consumed your friend's soul. The path to Zenith is through that darkness, not away from it. Now, go. Remember what you have seen. And remember that the Fold never gives without taking."

A path of shimmering violet light appeared before Luca, a beacon of hope leading into the Fold's lingering darkness. With a new understanding and a heavy heart, he began to walk. He awoke with a gasp, his eyes snapping open to the familiar, tense Sanctum. He looked down at his hand. The Hollowmark, once an invisible brand, now glowed with a steady, resonant violet light. He rose slowly, the weight of a lost history on his shoulders. He looked at Iris, at Riven, at the leaders of his world, and he knew his purpose.

He spoke one word, a promise to them all, and a command to himself.

"Zenith."

# Chapter 12: The Unspoken Accord

"*Courage is not the absence of fear, but the decision that something else is more important.*"

The Head's Sanctum had not changed, yet in the wake of Luca's return from the Aetherfold, nothing felt the same. The orb's ominous glow was gone, but the air itself still buzzed faintly, as though it struggled to settle after the truths it had been forced to witness. The crystal walls, usually a comforting, steady blue, seemed to reflect the shaken faces within, turning their fear and resolve into shimmering, distorted portraits. The silence that reigned was dense with meaning, a quiet stretched thin over the last twenty-four hours of chaos and revelation.

Luca sat up on the low cot, every movement deliberate, heavy, as if he were rising through invisible water. His body bore no wounds from his psychic journey, but his soul felt ancient, bruised by the weight of a history he now carried. The Hollowmark on his palm pulsed with a faint, deep violet-red rhythm—a second heartbeat not his own, a living echo of the Fold's touch. His eyes, when they met the worried gazes of his friends and leaders, were no longer the uncertain eyes of a boy. They were haunted, hollowed by what they had seen, yet brimming with a new, terrifying, and urgent clarity.

"It wasn't just a vision," he said quietly, his voice raw, as if scraped by the truths he'd witnessed. "It was memory. *Living* memory. The Soulstream itself, laid bare for me to see."

He recounted his journey, his words painting a vivid, horrifying picture. He spoke of Viralith, not as a one-dimensional monster, but as a man, a genius of Maritua's first era, warped by an unbearable, world-shattering grief. He described the birth of their island in the year 2037, a living entity that had consciously rejected the cold technology of its past. And he spoke of the prophecy, of the five legends—four students and one creature of pure magic—destined to stand against the coming darkness.

Finally, he looked at them, his gaze piercing. "Zenith isn't missing," he said, the words landing with the weight of a final verdict. "He's on Floor 300. The Fold called to him. It fed on his despair, his pain after the Selection. That's where the seal is weakest. That's where Viralith... *waits*."

The name, spoken aloud, seemed to stretch the shadows in the room. Orion closed his eyes, his knuckles white where he gripped his staff. Pepo's face was a mask of stone, his regal features burdened by the crushing realization of his predecessors' flawed, secret pact.

But it was Iris who moved first. She rose slowly, her own knuckles white as her nails bit into her palms. Her tear-streaked face, once a portrait of pure grief, was now hardening into a mask of cold, unyielding fury. She whispered to no one in particular, her voice a low, burning vow, "They erased Kaelin. They twisted Zenith." For a fleeting, agonizing second, a vivid image of Kaelin's smiling face, then her body dissolving into a cascade of gray ash, flickered behind Iris's eyes, a fresh, stabbing wound of grief. She squeezed her eyes shut, then opened them again, the fire within them hotter than ever.

"We're going down there," she said, her voice louder now, steadier, resonating with a fierce, unbreakable determination—a silent promise to the memory of her friend. "Even if the Fold itself tries to stop us."

Lyra stepped beside her, placing a hand gently on Iris's shoulder—not to calm her, but to share in that righteous anger. Her healing aura, usually a soft gold, pulsed with a brighter, more intense light.

Luca, seeing her resolve, felt his own solidify. He stepped forward, assuming a mantle of leadership he never wanted but now could not refuse. The Hollowmark on his hand glowed brighter, as if in agreement. "We find Zenith. We stop Viralith. And we locate the fifth legend, Glitch. In that order. The Fold is already stirring. There's no more time for fear."

Riven, who had been leaning against the far wall, a silent, brooding sentinel, pushed himself off the stone with a soft exhale. His gaze was sharp, calculating, his own personal grief a locked room no one else could enter. "The Fold owes me answers," he murmured, the words a cold promise, not a plea.

Nilo, who had been quietly observing, stepped into the light, brushing a piece of imaginary dust from his sleeve. He looked from Luca's glowing hand to Iris's furious eyes and sighed dramatically. "Well, if I'm going to die horribly in a nightmarish memory dimension, I suppose I'd like for it to be historically inconvenient for the forces of darkness. You can count me in." His humor, a thin but welcome veneer over a clear understanding of the peril, was a familiar, grounding presence.

The Unspoken Accord was made. They were no longer just students. They were a fellowship, bound by loss and a desperate, terrifying purpose.

The next twenty-four hours were a blur of intense, desperate preparation. The secluded training grounds on Floor 266, usually filled with the sounds of routine practice, now echoed with a new kind of energy—focused, sharp, and born of grim necessity.

Guided by Orion, Luca pushed past his physical and mental exhaustion, learning to control the Hollowmark. He practiced not casting spells, but attuning to the island's ley-lines, feeling for the faint, unsettling thread of Zenith's corrupted energy. He clutched the focus amulet Lyra had given him, a steady warmth in his palm, and learned to use his own fear not as a weakness, but as a compass needle, pointing him toward the greater despair that had consumed his friend. "I can feel it," he'd muttered to Orion, sweat trailing down his brow. "It's... it's not just a shimmer anymore. It's a voice. Zenith's voice... but it's wrong. It sounds like he's screaming through static."

Iris's training was a brutal, beautiful storm. Her mimicry magic, fueled by her cold, controlled fury, became faster, more precise. She practiced not just deflecting attacks, but seizing control of corrupted energy, twisting it, and turning it back on itself. She fought with Kaelin's broken pendant clutched in her fist, her every move a testament to her unyielding will to find answers and exact retribution.

Riven, meanwhile, prepared in solitude. He sharpened his whisper-thin blade with methodical calm, the rasp of steel on stone a low, meditative hum. He practiced his Chrono-flickers relentlessly, not just for combat, but for navigating the unpredictable, time-bending spaces he knew they would face in the Fold. His movements became even more fluid, hinting at a deeper, evolving power—a new trick with his temporal magic that promised both mastery and peril.

And Nilo was in his element. In a specialized arcane lab, surrounded by glowing diagrams and whirring, half-finished devices, he worked with a manic genius. He devised specialized tools for their mission: a compass that didn't point north, but tracked primal energy signatures, which he hoped would lead them to Glitch; a set of memory-stabilizer beacons designed to anchor them in the Fold's chaotic, shifting reality; and a unique signal jammer he theorized could disrupt psychic attacks by broadcasting a frequency of pure, mathematical nonsense.

Finally, they were ready. They gathered their gear—specialized ley-crystals, purified water, concentrated energy rations—and descended. They moved past the humming labs and libraries, past the silent training grounds, deeper and deeper into the sub-levels of the academy, where the air grew colder and the light grew thin.

The entrance to Floor 300 was nothing like they expected. There were no grand stairs, no ornate, sealed doors. It was just a low, jagged archway carved from raw, obsidian-like stone, which seemed to drink the light from their torches. The archway itself flickered with a faint, sickly violet shimmer. The air here felt heavy, ancient, and unnervingly *aware*.

Pepo, Orion, and Lyra stood before the gateway with them, their faces solemn, etched with the weight of Maritua's history.

"The fate of our world now rests on your courage," Pepo said, his voice devoid of its usual warmth, replaced by a grim resolve. "Remember the true meaning of balance."

Orion offered a final, tactical warning. "The Fold will prey on your minds. It will turn your own memories against you. Trust the stabilizers. Trust each other. But most of all, trust your purpose."

Lyra said nothing, but she stepped forward and touched each of them on the forehead, leaving behind a final, protective aura that felt like a whisper of home, a fragile shield against the encroaching despair.

Luca took a deep breath and looked at his team. Iris, her face set like stone, her hand never leaving the pendant at her throat. Riven, his eyes like steel, his presence a quiet, deadly calm. Nilo, his usual smirk replaced by a grim determination, a small, intricate device clutched in his hand. Luca touched his own Hollowmark, feeling its steady, violet glow against his skin, anchoring him. He nodded once to Pepo, a silent vow to carry the burden they had been given.

He took his final step toward the archway, his heart pounding not from fear, but from something deeper—purpose. The Fold hummed in reply, the violet light brightening, beckoning them into its depths.

Then—the island *screamed*.

A terrifying, island-wide alarm shrieked through Nebula, a sound no living student had ever heard before. It was not the quiet alarm of a breached security ward, but the full, blaring, red-alert of Maritua under siege. The ground under their feet didn't just tremble; it quaked with the rhythm of distant, concussive blasts. The crystal walls of the ancient sub-level began to shudder, dust and stone raining down from the ceiling.

Over the blaring alarms, a voice—distorted by static but grimly clear—boomed from Pepo's glowing command crystal. "Crystals shattering in all sectors! Frostvale's outer walls are breached! Nebula is compromised! CODE RED! ALL REALMS ARE UNDER ATTACK! LAZHERAK'S FORCES ARE OVERWHELMING ALL DEFENSES!"

Pepo's face, already etched with worry, turned ashen. Orion's eyes widened, a silent, shared horror passing between him and the Pinnacle. The urgency for the Fold, the mission to save Zenith, was instantly and brutally superseded by the reality of their home burning around them.

"The Fold must wait!" Pepo barked, his voice strained, raw with a newly awakened fury that was terrifying to behold. "Maritua first! You are needed on the surface! Now!" He gestured wildly to the nearest exit from the sub-level, away from the waiting archway.

The team didn't enter the Fold. They didn't have a choice. They turned and scrambled back towards the chaos, the sounds of a desperate, losing battle drawing closer with every second. Their meticulously planned mission into the abyss had been violently interrupted by a far more immediate and devastating threat.

Behind them, the archway to the Fold, silent and patient, pulsed with its malevolent violet light.

And above them, on the surface, Maritua screamed as it burned.

# Chapter 13: Where Shadows Rise

*"The world remembers its wounds. And some wounds, once opened, never truly heal."*

They burst from the oppressive quiet of the sub-levels into a hammer-blow of sound and fury. The world had gone mad.

**Nebula, Maritua's gleaming heart, was a city under siege**. The sky, once a vibrant canvas of magical light and soaring sky-whale migrations, was now choked with oily black smoke and spiraling vortices of corrupted, violet energy that tore at the very fabric of the air. The elegant blink-platforms, the ribbons of light that were the city's veins, lay shattered, their light-strands severed, their broken husks plunging from the sky like fallen, weeping stars. The air tasted of ozone, burning crystal, and the hot, metallic tang of fresh blood. The academy's alarm was no longer a shriek; it was a constant, desperate groan, drowned out by the screams of Maritua itself.

A legion born of forgotten grief and twisted memory surged through the crystalline streets. But this was no unthinking, shuffling horde. This was an army, and it had generals. Leading the assault were Viralith's other partners, a grim and powerful council of despair, each a master of a different form of magical warfare.

Luca saw him first:

**Moros, the Chronos-Weaver**, a spectral blur of fractured time, his form flickering in and out of existence. He moved not just through space but through moments, his presence making allied defenders move as if through thick mud, while the corrupted forces under his command blurred with unnatural speed. He was a living paradox, turning the battle into an impossible dance against an invisible opponent.

Beside him moved

**Thanatos, the Soul-Drinker**, a gaunt, skeletal figure whose eyes glowed with a malevolent, siphoning green light. He fought with a terrifying drain, sucking the very life and magical essence from those he touched. The more magic Thanatos consumed, the more powerful he became, a walking embodiment of the Pact of the Pale Flame.

And weaving through the chaos like a wisp of sentient smoke was

**Erebus, the Shadow-Lurker**, a master of illusions and psychological warfare. His form shifted like a wisp of smoke, a living reflection of despair. He conjured horrors from his enemies' minds, showing them their deepest fears and regrets, turning hope into fear. He was a master of psychological warfare, making the battle a fight for sanity itself.

"They're targeting the ley-line confluences!" Orion's voice, amplified by a desperate spell, cut through the chaos from a distant command center. "If they sever Nebula's core connection, the island will fall!"

Pepo, his crimson robes now streaked with dust, moved with a grim authority. "Vega! Glint! Elderon! Secure the outer sectors! The Nexus Core is our last stand! We cannot allow them to reach the heart!" The Sector Lords, battered but resolute, vanished into the maelstrom, their unique magics flaring to meet the overwhelming tide.

Luca, Iris, and Riven plunged into the fray. Their planned, surgical strike into the Fold had become a desperate, chaotic brawl for survival. Iris's rage fueled her mimicry, Riven's Chrono-flickers became a blur of lethal precision, and Luca's Hollowmark was a conduit of raw, disruptive energy, unbalancing the hordes. But for every one they struck down, ten more rose.

Across Maritua, the other realms were bleeding. The crisis was a systemic assault, tailored to each realm's deepest fears. In

**Frostvale**, Vega fought **Moros** as her own ice shattered, turned into weapons by his psychic scream. In

**Dravemire**, Glint was besieged by **Thanatos**, whose siphoning light drained his strength with every blow. In

**Viridawn**, Elderon watched his tree-cities wither under the assault of **Erebus**, whose illusions poisoned his forests with despair. In

**Lunareth**, Lyra fought alongside her students against **Anteros**, a horrifying echo of lost loved ones, turning solace into a weapon.

Back in Nebula, the battle around Luca's team intensified. They were pushed relentlessly towards the base of Nebula Tower, a primary ley-line confluence. The air crackled with raw, malevolent power. A skeletal figure radiating triumph,

**Lazherak**, manifested directly at the confluence. He wasn't just fighting; he was orchestrating a ritual. He raised his bone-staff, and the very ley-lines beneath Nebula began to pulse, like veins draining color from the world. The light of Nebula itself seemed to dim, its vibrant glow flickering as if life was being siphoned from its core.

He named the ritual, his voice a chilling incantation: "The Echo Severance!"

Luca's team was forced into a desperate confrontation, pushing their powers to their absolute limits to disrupt the ritual. Luca's Hollowmark throbbed, pulsing violet, resonating with the Soulstream. He slammed his hands down, sending disruptive pulses to protect Maritua's very heart. He could feel the island's pain, a deep, cosmic wound that mirrored his own, and in the chaos, he heard a fractured whisper—Zenith's voice, raw with anguish, screaming through static. The sound made him falter for a heartbeat, a terrifying, personal crack in the chaos.

Iris's magic, fueled by a cold, controlled fury, was a beautiful and terrifying thing to witness. Her mimicry loops wove through the corrupted hordes, not just reflecting their attacks but twisting them. A wave of bone-shards flew towards her; she twisted it, amplifying the force and shattering a dozen undead. But as she fought, a corrupted student, a boy she'd shared a laugh with, lunged with a rusted blade. Iris's grief turned to a cold, focused fury. The phantom image of Kaelin's face, smiling and then gone, filled her vision. A guttural sob tore from her throat. Her magic surged, reflecting its own decay back upon it, accelerating its disintegration into dust. "You will not defile this place!" she screamed, her voice raw, a primal cry against the desecration of memory.

Riven was a blur of Chrono-flickers, a silver ghost in the chaos. He moved through time itself, appearing and disappearing. But for a moment, as he fought, he saw a vision of himself from the Trial of Succession—younger, bleeding, his blade shattered, a sense of crushing powerlessness. He pushed past the memory, turning the humiliation of a past defeat into lethal precision, his movements now fueled by a desperate need to not fail again.

Nilo, his face grim, worked frantically with his devices, searching for a mathematical flaw in the madness. His tech was a furious, sparking testament to his ingenuity against the impossible. The corrupted forces flooded the nexus, overwhelming defenses. The Sector Lords relayed their final, desperate pleas through Pepo's crystal, their voices ragged.

Lazherak raised his staff, its bony tip crackling with the siphoned energy of the island, ready to deliver the final, severing blow that would plunge Nebula into darkness forever. The heroes were moments from being overrun. All hope was lost.

It was then that Master Selix, his face a mask of blood and grim resolve, saw the one, desperate path to victory. He saw the stalemate, the fading strength of his students, and the unstoppable ritual. And he made his choice.

"Knowledge protects," he said, his voice quiet but carrying with an unshakeable finality. He took a single, deliberate step forward into the open. "And the greatest knowledge... is knowing the price of victory."

He did not run. He did not charge. He stopped twenty feet from the swirling vortex of corrupted energy and began to cast.

"Master, no!" Iris screamed, recognizing the terrifying build-up of energy.

It was too late. Selix's hands began to weave a complex glyph that none of them had ever seen in any textbook. It pulsed with a blinding, self-consuming light, and the air around him began to hiss and warp. It was a **"Final Word**

**Glyph,"** a legendary and forbidden spell that converts the caster's entire life force—their magic, their memories, their very soul—into a single, targeted burst of pure, unmaking energy.

It was an agonizing process. The light didn't just emanate from his hands; it burst from within him. Cracks of pure white energy traced across his skin like lightning trapped under glass. Light poured from his eyes, no longer seeing the battlefield, but something beyond. He grunted, his body trembling violently, straining to contain the power of his own unmaking. This wasn't a quick leap; it was a slow, deliberate act of self-annihilation, guided by an iron will.

"A lesson is not taught until it is learned!" he roared, his voice no longer that of a man, but of a detonating star. He raised his head, his gaze fixed on Lazherak.

**"This is for the students you twisted!"**

With a final, soul-shattering cry, he did not jump. He **unleashed** himself. His body erupted in a focused, horizontal beam of pure, white-hot order that slammed into the central conduit of the ritual.

For a moment, there was no sound, only light. The violet corruption of the ritual was overwhelmed, consumed by the brilliant, purifying star of Selix's being. The conduit didn't just stall; it violently recoiled. A psychic backlash of pure, ordered energy erupted from the point of impact, striking Lazherak like an invisible battering ram. He was thrown back, a shriek of genuine pain tearing from him as his concentration shattered, the complex glyphs of his ritual fracturing in the air.

The beam of light faded, its purpose fulfilled. Where Master Selix had stood, nothing remained but a faint, shimmering heat and a single, perfect crystal shard that fell and chimed once against the stone before dissolving. His body had been the fuel, and it was utterly spent. The ritual was not stopped, but it was critically flawed, the nexus now permanently poisoned against the Fold's influence by the lingering echo of his sacrifice.

Lazherak snarled, clutching his head from the psychic shockwave. **"A futile gesture!"** he spat, though his voice now held a new edge of fury and his focus was broken.

It was not a futile gesture. It was a checkmate. Master Selix had sacrificed his most powerful piece to create an opening. And he had just given his students—stunned, grief-stricken, but alive—one final, desperate chance to win the war.

The fighting continued. The Phantom, his power flickering, engaged Lazherak directly, his crimson glow a beacon against the darkness. But for every bone he unmade, a new one formed. The battle was a draw, a stalemate of raw, unyielding will against an endless tide.

And as the battle raged, something else began to happen. The Nexus Core, weakened and frayed, began to pulse erratically. Not with a hum, but with a deep, resonant

**thrum**. A sound that came from the very depths of the island. A sound that Luca's Hollowmark, burning on his palm, echoed in perfect sync.

The ground around the nexus, still slick with blood and ash, began to crack. Not from a spell, but from pressure building beneath the earth, a sound like a coffin lid groaning open. The cracks glowed with a sickening, violet-black light.

All eyes—Phantom's, Lazherak's, the Sector Lords', the heroes'—snapped to the ground. The fight stopped. Lazherak, for the first time, looked not triumphant, but ecstatic. The Phantom, his crimson glow dimming, looked utterly horrified.

From the glowing cracks, a voice—a single, powerful, resonating voice—began to rise. It was not a whisper. It was not a scream. It was a chord. A perfect, harmonious chord that vibrated through the very bones of the island, a sound of profound power and ancient majesty.

The heroes felt it in their bones, a chilling resonance that threatened to shatter their very souls. And then, from the depths of Floor 300, a new light pierced the darkness. A light that was not a glow, but a presence. A light that was not a color, but a memory.

The seal was broken. The Accord of Silence, shattered. From the depths of the island, an ancient will had awakened, a chilling, triumphant presence poised to consume the world.

As the light flared, Luca caught a fleeting, horrific glimpse of a shadow version of Maritua—a world of ash and bone, a landscape of despair. His mind screamed a single, desperate thought: "No... it can't be him."

The true battle had just begun. But the war... the war was already lost.

# Chapter 14: The Heart of the Fold

"*The cruelest prison is the one we build for ourselves, wall by wall, from the stones of our own pride.*"

The harmonious chord rising from the cracked earth of the Nexus did not fade. It swelled, a sound of profound power that washed over the battlefield, silencing the screams and the clash of steel with its chilling, serene majesty. The violet light from the fissures intensified, not as a chaotic surge, but as a controlled, deliberate, and impossibly beautiful dawn. The remaining corrupted husks on the battlefield froze, then turned to dust, their purpose fulfilled.

Across the ruined Nexus, Lazherak's skeletal face, alight with ecstatic reverence, turned towards the light. He fell to one knee. In the distance, the fighting across Nebula ceased. The spectral form of Moros, the Chronos-Weaver, solidified from a blur of fractured time and bowed his head. Thanatos, the Soul-Drinker, paused his life-draining assault and knelt amidst his withered victims. Erebus, the Shadow-Lurker, let his terrifying illusions dissolve into harmless smoke as he, too, showed silent, absolute deference. The entire army of the dead, across the entire city, stopped its rampage and knelt as one.

The Red Phantom stood poised, his crimson form a stark silhouette of dread, his stillness a silent scream against the coming apocalypse.

And from the heart of the light, a figure rose.

It was not the skeletal form of Viralith from the legends. It was not a monster of shadow and bone. It was Zenith Cael.

He ascended from the ground, his feet never touching the stone, his body moving with an unnatural, impossible grace. His academy uniform was pristine, unmarred by the battle that had just laid waste to their world. But his eyes... his eyes were not his own. They glowed with that same harmonious, terrifying violet light, ancient and all-knowing. A faint, sad smile touched his lips, a smile of serene, absolute power. His voice, when he spoke, was a layered chord, Zenith's familiar tone woven through a deeper, older, and infinitely more powerful resonance that vibrated in the very air.

"Be still," the voice said, and the very wind obeyed. The dust settled. The fires ceased their roaring. "The pain is over."

He turned his gaze to the skeletal form of his most loyal servant. "Rise, Lazherak. You have done well." He then looked upon the assembled heroes, the Sector Lords, and the lone, crimson guardian. He swept a hand across the devastation, a gesture not of triumph, but of profound disappointment. "All this struggle. All this suffering. A testament to a flawed design."

The figure's smile tightened for a fraction of a second as he touched a hand to Zenith's chest. A flicker of brilliant, pure white light—the defiant echo of Master Selix's sacrifice—resisted him from within, a tiny star of ordered magic refusing to be extinguished.

"This vessel... it is the finest I have found in a century, a perfect symphony of pride and despair," the being mused, his voice tinged with a faint, cosmic annoyance. "And yet, an old man's dying breath left a... discordance. An impurity in the otherwise perfect silence. The possession is incomplete, the final anchor not yet set. No matter. Even a flawed masterpiece is a masterpiece still. It is enough."

His glowing eyes swept over them, and in that gaze, they felt the weight of an ancient, inconsolable grief.

**"I am Viralith."**

As the name was spoken, a wave of pure psychic pressure washed over the battlefield, forcing everyone, hero and healer alike, to stumble. Lazherak, Moros, Thanatos, and Erebus all bowed their heads lower in a single, synchronized motion of utter fealty. This was their god.

Iris gasped, her hand flying to her mouth. "Zenith...?"

"The person you knew as Zenith is at peace," Viralith replied, his gaze sweeping over them, not with malice, but with a vast, heartbreaking pity. "He has given himself to a cause greater than his own pain. As you all will. I have come not to destroy your world, but to save it from itself."

This was his vessel. Not a desecrated corpse, but a perfect, living anchor, willingly given in a moment of profound despair.

As he spoke, a new horror began. The world started to bleed its color. A creeping grayness spread from his feet, silencing the vibrant hues of Maritua. The brilliant crystal of Nebula's towers began to dull, the shimmering magic within them quieting. The sky above began to lose its depth, looking less like a living expanse and more like a fixed, painted backdrop. He was not just speaking of his perfect world; he was actively imposing it, overwriting their chaotic, beautiful reality with the sterile, unchanging perfection of the Fold.

"For centuries, I have watched," Viralith continued, his calm voice a terrifying counterpoint to the silent destruction he was unleashing. "I have watched this beautiful, chaotic island tear itself apart with grief and loss. This cycle of suffering, of impermanence... it is a flaw in creation. A wound that never heals."

He extended a hand, and the very air around Iris shimmered. For a single, breathtaking moment, the ruins around her were replaced by a sun-drenched meadow. Kaelin was there, whole and vibrant, weaving flowers into a chain, and she looked up and smiled, her real smile, the one that crinkled her eyes. "See, Iris?" Viralith's voice whispered. "In my world, nothing is ever truly lost. I offer you the memory without the hurt. Is that not mercy?"

The illusion shattered, leaving Iris gasping, fresh tears streaming down her face.

He turned to Riven. "I have felt the sting of your failure, Last Ash. The moment time broke for you." The battlefield dissolved into a vision of a younger Riven, his blade shattered, kneeling in defeat before Pepo. "I can unwrite that page. I can give you the victory you were denied."

His glowing eyes finally settled on Luca. "And you, the Keystone. In my world, there is no failure, because there is no change. You will never have to fear being too late again."

The temptation was a sweet, insidious poison. But it was Luca who found his voice first, the lessons of the Aetherfold burning in his mind.

"That's not life," Luca said, his voice shaking but firm. "That's a cage. A beautiful cage, but still a prison. Loss is what gives our choices meaning. Without it, we're not alive."

"Without it, we are at peace!" Viralith countered, the first flicker of his ancient grief flashing in his eyes.

Iris, her face a mask of renewed fury at the vile twisting of Kaelin's memory, screamed, "You call that peace? You would make us all ghosts in your perfect museum! Kaelin chose to be brave! You want to steal that choice from everyone!"

Viralith's sad smile faded. "So be it. The stubbornness of life is its greatest flaw. A flaw I will correct."

The battle began. But it was unlike any they had fought before. Viralith didn't just cast spells; he conducted a symphony of despair. At his silent command, Moros, Thanatos, and Erebus re-engaged, their attacks now perfectly synchronized with the psychic horrors he conjured. The heroes were now fighting on two fronts: the physical threat of the lieutenants and the psychic/emotional threat of Viralith himself.

But Maritua's own guardians answered. From a hidden sanctum deep within the High Tower, **The Weaver** felt the fabric of reality fraying. Before her was not a loom of thread, but of light, its strands the very ley-lines and concepts that made up Nebula. As Viralith's grayness spread, she seized the golden threads of "courage" and "hope," furiously re-weaving them back into the city's metaphysical tapestry, a desperate, defiant act of creation against his unmaking.

On the battlefield, **The Whisper** moved. They saw Erebus conjuring a phantasm of a fallen guardian to demoralize the city's defenders. The Whisper didn't attack. They simply placed a hand on the phantasm's shadow and *pulled*. The concept of "fear" was stolen from the illusion for three crucial seconds. The terrifying specter suddenly looked confused, benign, and its power over the defenders shattered, leaving Erebus momentarily disoriented by the psychic backlash.

Even so, they were fading. Viralith was too strong, his control over the Fold absolute. And Luca knew what he had to do. He wasn't meant to fight the storm. He was meant to be its eye.

"Cover me!" he yelled. He looked at the serene, possessed form of his friend. "I'm not fighting you, Viralith. I'm here for him!"

Closing his eyes, Luca pushed his consciousness through the Hollowmark, not outward, but inward. He followed the thin, screaming thread of Zenith's despair, diving headfirst into the prison of his friend's mind.

The world shifted from the chaos of the battlefield to a landscape of cold, perfect order. Luca stood in a vast, empty throne room. Thewalls were made of flawless, polished ice that whispered Zenith's deepest insecurities. A single, ornate throne sat upon a high dais. Seated on the throne was Zenith. He wore a crown of black ice, and he was staring at his own reflection in the polished floor, a look of profound, lonely misery on his face. Spectral figures moved in the shadows around him—a stern, disapproving image of his father, a crowd of whispering students mocking his "incomplete" resonance, a vision of Luca accepting the accolades Zenith believed were his by right. This was the hell his own pride had built.

"Zenith!" Luca called out.

The crowned figure looked up, his eyes hollow. *"You shouldn't be here,"* the dream-Zenith whispered. *"This is my kingdom. The kingdom of failure."*

"This isn't a kingdom, Zenith, it's a prison!" Luca said, walking forward, his steps echoing in the vast, cold space. "Viralith is using you, feeding on this despair."

*"I deserve it,"* Zenith replied, not looking at him. *"I failed. You were the one they chose."*

"They chose me because I'm a mess!" Luca almost shouted, the words raw and honest. "They chose me because I'm full of cracks, and that's how the light gets in! Your resonance wasn't incomplete because you were weak. It was incomplete because you were fighting yourself! You were trying so hard to be perfect that you forgot how to be whole."

Luca stood before the throne now, his hand outstretched. "Iris is out there, getting torn apart for you. Riven and Nilo are fighting for you. The Red Phantom is fighting for you. I'm here for you. We are your friends. That's more real than any of these shadows." He pointed to the specter of Zenith's father. "Your worth isn't measured by anyone else's approval, Zenith. Not his. Not mine. It's measured by your own heart. Come home."

The dream-Zenith looked from the accusing shadows to Luca's outstretched hand. A crack appeared in the icy throne.

"We're not leaving you behind," Luca said, his voice soft now.

A single tear, hot and real, traced a path down the dream-Zenith's cold cheek. He looked at Luca, and for the first time, a flicker of his old, true self sparked in his eyes. Slowly, hesitantly, he reached out and took Luca's hand.

Back on the battlefield, the serene, all-powerful form of Viralith-Zenith suddenly convulsed. His eyes flickered, the harmonious violet light stuttering, replaced for a split second by Zenith's own terrified blue. The flaw left by Selix's sacrifice was being exploited from within. His power wavered.

Just then, as Viralith's reality-warping power flickered, an impossible thing happened. From the crystalline monument that was once Master Selix, a single drop of pure, untainted magic fell like a tear. Where it landed on the blood-soaked stone, a single, impossibly vibrant, rainbow-colored flower bloomed, pulsing with a light of pure, chaotic life before vanishing. Viralith recoiled, not from pain, but from disgust at this "imperfect" anomaly.

**"NOW!"** Riven roared, seizing the moment of distraction.

The Red Phantom, who had been waiting, struck. He didn't aim a killing blow. He placed his palm on Viralith-Zenith's forehead and unleashed a focused, contained pulse of his reality-ordering crimson energy. At the same time, Iris, Nilo, and Riven poured all their remaining power into a single, combined assault.

It was not an attack meant to destroy the body. It was an eviction notice for the soul.

## Chapter 15: The Unmaking

"*Perfection is a beautiful, sterile cage. True life is found in the glory of its flaws.*"

The eviction notice was served.

For a single, impossible heartbeat, the combined assault of the heroes—a symphony of righteous fury, temporal distortion, logical chaos, and pure, ordering will—struck the possessed form of Zenith Cael. The harmonious violet light in his eyes flickered violently, and Zenith's own true, terrified blue broke through like a drowning man gasping for air. The flaw left by Master Selix's sacrifice, a tiny seed of defiance, had been nurtured into a raging fire by Luca's psychic rescue. The perfect prison was cracking from within.

But a god does not surrender its throne so easily.

Viralith, the ancient soul of grief, recoiled not in pain, but in outrage. The serene, sad smile vanished from Zenith's face, replaced by a mask of cold, cosmic fury. A soundless scream erupted from him—not a sound of voice, but a psychic shockwave of pure, unadulterated despair. It was the collective agony of every memory the Fold had ever consumed, unleashed in a single, devastating wave.

"*ENOUGH!*"

The word was a physical blow. In the hidden heart of Nebula Tower, The Weaver cried out as the golden threads of "hope" on her conceptual loom snapped under the strain. In a ruined plaza, The Whisper, who had been trying to siphon the fear from a group of huddled civilians, was thrown back, overwhelmed by a tidal wave of pure despair that was too vast to be contained or redirected.

The wave slammed into the heroes, throwing them back like leaves in a hurricane. Iris cried out as the raw despair hit her, the memory of Kaelin's ash on her hands flaring into an almost unbearable pain. Riven was thrown through the air, his Chrono-flicker stuttering as the wave of absolute misery warped the flow of time around him. Nilo's devices sparked and died, overwhelmed by the sheer, illogical force of a billion sorrows.

The Red Phantom, the embodiment of order, took the brunt of the psychic blast. His crimson form flickered violently, the steady glow dimming as if starved of light. A visible crack, like splintering crimson glass, appeared on his featureless mask. He staggered back, a knee dropping to the scorched stone for the first time in centuries, his very essence wounded by the sheer magnitude of the chaos.

The wave of despair rolled on, striking the great central spire of Nebula. The ancient crystal, the very spine of the city, groaned under the strain. A web of deep, dark fractures spread up its length with a sound like the world breaking, scarring the heart of Maritua, a wound that would never fully heal.

Viralith had reasserted control. The violet light in Zenith's eyes no longer just glowed; it burned with a cold, absolute intensity. The flaw was still there, a dissonant hum beneath the perfect chord of his power, but he was now compensating with raw, overwhelming force. He rose higher into the air, the gray, color-draining aura of the Fold spreading from him faster than ever, turning the vibrant ruins into a monochrome wasteland.

"You cling to your beautiful, fleeting pain," Viralith's layered voice boomed, resonating with a final, sorrowful judgment. "I will give you an eternity to cherish it."

He raised a hand to deliver the final, world-ending blow. All hope seemed to extinguish with the fading colors.

It was then that Nilo, clutching a smoking, ruined compass in his hand, looked up with wide, incredulous eyes. The needle wasn't just spinning. It was vibrating so violently it was about to shatter, and it was pointing not at an enemy, not at a ley-line, but at the small, crystalline scar on the ground where Master Selix had unmade himself.

From that scar, a single point of light emerged. It was not white, not gold, not violet. It was every color and no color at all, a point of pure, joyful, chaotic potential. It was the island's unbound soul, finally awakened by the depth of its own wound.

The point of light did not explode. It giggled.

A sound like a thousand tiny, crystalline bells chiming at once filled the air, and from the light, *it* unfolded. It had no fixed form. One moment it was a shimmering, rainbow-hued hummingbird made of pure data; the next, a laughing fox with a tail of cascading musical notes; then a swirling vortex of happy, nonsensical geometric shapes. It was a living, breathing paradox. From his command center, Orion gasped, recognizing it from a single, redacted line in a forbidden text. It was the Fifth Legend. It was Glitch.

Glitch zipped through the air, leaving a trail of vibrant, life-affirming color that pushed back Viralith's encroaching grayness. It did not attack. It *played.* It swooped past Riven, and the fractured timeline around him didn't just stabilize; it sang. He saw not the failure of his past, but the infinite possibilities of his future. It danced around Iris, and the cold fire of her grief was not extinguished, but infused with a warm, fierce protectiveness. The memory of Kaelin was no longer just a weapon of rage; it was a shield of love.

Glitch then spiraled around Luca. The Hollowmark on his palm, the key to the Fold's despair, blazed not with violet, but with a brilliant, golden light. The echo of the Fold was silenced, and for the first time, he felt a pure, direct connection to the Soulstream, to the very heartbeat of Maritua. He was no longer just a keystone for a broken lock; he was a conduit for a living world.

Viralith stared, his divine composure finally cracking. This... this was an error. A bug in the system. An imperfection so profound it defied his understanding. "What... is this anomaly?"

"It's called life, you miserable ghost," Nilo yelled, a manic, triumphant grin spreading across his face. "And it's time for a system update!"

Zenith, from deep within the prison of his own mind, saw the shimmering, joyful light of Glitch. He saw his friends, battered but unbroken, infused with a new, impossible hope. And he found the final ounce of strength. He didn't just fight back. He *pushed.*

Luca felt it. He staggered to his feet, his mind reeling from the psychic assault, the Hollowmark on his palm a brand of burning gold. He saw Iris push herself up, her arm throbbing where she'd been thrown, her face a mask of beautiful, tear-streaked fury. Riven rose, a thin line of blood trickling from his temple, his temporal energy frayed but holding. Nilo, nursing a burn on his hand from his last exploding gadget, gave a shaky thumbs-up. They were broken, bleeding, but they were not beaten.

Luca raised his head, his eyes glowing with the golden light of the island. "He's with us! Now! We end this together!"

They formed a circle, a desperate, defiant ring of five around the god of despair. Glitch became the energy between them, a living thread of chaotic potential weaving their wills into one. Luca began the chant, his voice clear and strong, a declaration of war against sterile perfection.

"For the fear that teaches courage!" he cried, his voice resonating with the memory of his own crippling doubt.

Iris, her eyes blazing, her voice a testament to the friend she would never forget, added hers. "For the loss that proves we loved!"

Riven, his blade held steady, his gaze fixed on the path forward, spoke with the weight of a lifetime of regret, now unburdened. "For the past that shapes our future!"

Nilo, his mind alight with the beautiful, unsolvable equation of existence, shouted his part with a laugh. "For the question that seeks an answer!"

A new voice, cracked and raw but unmistakably real, tore through Viralith's layered drone. It was Zenith. His own hand, trembling, rose to mirror the others.

"For the flaw," he choked out, tears streaming down his face, "that makes us *whole*!"

The five declarations, the five fundamental truths of a messy, beautiful, imperfect life, merged. The Weaver felt the new pattern and wove it into the tapestry of reality with a triumphant cry. The Sector Lords watched in awe, their own immense power paling in comparison to the conceptual weapon being forged before them. Glitch pulsed, unleashing their combined will not as a beam of force, but as an overwhelming wave of pure, unadulterated *life*. It was the feeling of a first laugh, the warmth of a shared memory, the sting of a scraped knee, the quiet joy of a sunset, the bittersweet pain of a goodbye—a billion chaotic, contradictory, wonderful moments all at once.

The wave of life washed over Viralith.

He did not scream. He did not burn. He was simply... overwhelmed. His perfect, sterile order, his world of silent, unchanging memory, could not process the infinite, messy complexity of reality. It was like showing a perfect circle an impossible, fractal shape. His logic shattered.

The possession broke.

With a final, shuddering gasp, the ancient, grieving soul of Viralith was torn from Zenith's body. For a fleeting moment, the heroes saw his true form—a translucent, spectral figure of a man in scholar's robes, his face etched with millennia of sorrow. He looked not at them, but past them, as if seeing the family he had lost so long ago. He looked tired.

Then, the Fold, his own creation, claimed him. The violet light collapsed inward, pulling him back not as its ruler, but as just another sad, weeping echo in its silent halls. The gateway sealed, and the light was gone.

As their god vanished, the source of his lieutenants' power was severed. On the battlefield, Lazherak, Moros, Thanatos, and Erebus looked up in confusion, their borrowed time expiring. They did not scream or fight. They simply crumbled, their forms dissolving into piles of fine, gray ash, finally granted the peace of true oblivion.

The war was over.

Zenith Cael fell from the sky, his body limp. Iris caught him before he hit the ground, holding him tight, her tears of grief finally mixing with tears of relief as she lowered him gently to the scorched stone.

The world was silent. In that stillness, Glitch did one last, playful loop around the exhausted heroes. It left a single, shimmering petal of impossible color on Zenith's still chest—a final gift of chaotic life. Then, with a sound like a fading, happy chime, it dissolved back into the light of the healing island, its purpose served.

The magical quiet faded, replaced by the whisper of the wind through the shattered spires and the distant groan of settling crystal. The adrenaline was gone, leaving behind an exhaustion so deep it felt etched into their bones. They stood in the ruins of their home, surrounded by the evidence of their victory and its terrible price.

As the petal on his chest pulsed with a soft, warm light, Zenith coughed, his eyes fluttering open. The harmonious violet was gone, replaced by his own familiar, terrified blue. He looked up at Iris, then at the devastation around them, and a look of profound shame washed over his face. "Iris... I..." he choked out, the words catching in his throat.

"It's okay," she whispered, her voice cracking. "It's over. You're home."

Luca knelt beside them, placing a steadying hand on Zenith's shoulder. Their eyes met, and in that single look, years of rivalry, resentment, and misunderstanding dissolved into a simple, profound truth: they were brothers, bound by the fire they had just walked through.

Riven sheathed his blade, the sound a quiet, final click in the stillness. He stood over them, not as a mysterious outsider, but as a silent, watchful guardian. Nilo sagged against a broken pillar, his usual smirk gone, replaced by a look of weary, awestruck relief. He gave a shaky thumbs-up that conveyed more than words ever could.

Luca looked from the faces of his friends—his family—to the horizon, where the first hints of a real dawn were beginning to break through the smoke-choked sky. The city was scarred. They were all scarred. But they were alive, and they were together.

The war was over. Now, the healing could begin.

# EPILOGUE

A full season had passed. The sky above Nebula was no longer choked with smoke, but scarred with the silver threads of newly-woven blink-platforms. The city was healing, its wounds slowly closing over with the stubborn, brilliant magic of a world that refused to stay broken.

They stood together at the Whispering Glass, the fractured dome of silvered stone catching the light of the setting sun . The five of them. It was the first time they had all returned here since the beginning.

Iris's hand rested on the twin to Kaelin's pendant at her throat, the metal warm against her skin. The ache of her friend's absence was still there, a quiet, hollow space in her heart, but it no longer burned with rage. Now, it was a gentle fire—a constant reminder of the price of love, and the strength found in refusing to let a memory die.

Beside her, Riven stood with his arms uncrossed for once, his gaze fixed on the horizon. He watched a flock of Whispergulls chase the fading light, and for the first time since anyone could remember, a small, genuine smile touched the corner of his lips. The shadows in his past had not vanished, but he no longer stood within them.

Zenith watched the reflection of the sky in the mirrored stone, his own face looking back, clear and calm. He had been chosen by Viralith as a perfect vessel of pride and despair. He now understood that the despair was a poison, but the pride—the desperate need to be worthy—had been the very thing that allowed him to hear his friends' voices in the dark. It was the flaw that had become his salvation.

"You know," Nilo said, breaking the comfortable silence as he tried to polish a smudge off the reflective rock with his sleeve, "being a 'Legend of the New Era' is exhausting. The official portraits are a nightmare, and you wouldn't believe the paperwork. I specifically requested we be designated as 'Saviors, Class One, with pension options.' They're still debating it."

Iris chuckled, a sound as bright and clear as it had ever been. "I don't think 'normal' was ever in the cards for us, Nilo."

"Normal? Who wants normal?" Luca replied, a quiet confidence in his voice that felt entirely his own. He felt the steady, peaceful hum of the Soulstream not as an external force, but as a gentle rhythm within his own chest. He was no longer just a boy on a living island; he was a part of its song.

He looked at their reflections. He saw the four of them—himself, Iris, Riven, and Nilo—etched against the sunset. But behind them, woven through their images like a thread of impossible light, the sky in the mirror shimmered with a joyful, chaotic energy. It was a fifth presence, formless and vibrant. It was Glitch.

Zenith's reflection stood beside Luca's, solid and whole, separate from that shimmering light. A hero forged in the fire, standing with the legends.

"The prophecy was always for five," Luca said quietly, a sense of awe washing over him. "Four of us, and the island's soul." He turned to Zenith, a look of profound understanding passing between them. "It never said there couldn't be a hero standing beside us."

Zenith nodded, his own quiet strength a testament to the long road he had walked back to himself.

Luca reached out and traced the feather sigil in the stone, the one that had once terrified him with its impossible familiarity . It no longer felt like a brand of a forgotten past, but a promise. A promise that even the deepest wounds could become a map to find your way home.

"No," Luca said, answering Iris's earlier comment, his voice full of a hard-won peace. "Not normal. Better."

And as the four human legends and the hero who had saved himself stood watching the sun bleed into the sea, they felt their fifth companion all around them—in the impossible colors of the sky, in the wild beauty of the wind, in the beautiful, chaotic, and imperfect silence of a world that was wounded, but finally, truly, whole. Maritua was singing again. And this time, they all knew the words.

9 788198 854162

Printed at Repro India Ltd.